Little Croker

'A welcome addition to sports literature for youngsters.'
Sunday Independent

'One young sports obsessive I know sped through the story.'
The Irish Times

'Young GAA fans everywhere will want to get their hands on a
copy of *Little Croker*.'
Carlow Nationalist

'Full of football action, talk of tactics and the highs and lows of the
game, this will hit the right chord with young footballers.'
The Evening Echo

'O'Brien is good at conjuring up the atmosphere of the GAA and
the importance that a club has in a local community. Will appeal to
football-mad boys and girls.'
Books Ireland

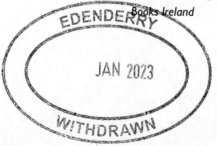
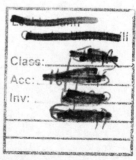

JOE O'BRIEN is an award-winning gardener who lives in Ballyfermot, Dublin. He is the author of three books about GAA player, Danny Wilde: *Little Croker*, *Féile Fever* and *Tiger Boots*. He is also the author of *Beyond the Cherry Tree* and the popular *Alfie Green* series for younger readers.

Little Croker

Joe O'Brien

THE O'BRIEN PRESS
DUBLIN

First published 2008 by The O'Brien Press Ltd,
12 Terenure Road East, Rathgar, Dublin 6, Ireland.
Tel: +353 1 4923333; Fax: +353 1 4922777
E-mail: books@obrien.ie; Website: www.obrien.ie
Reprinted 2009, 2011, 2014.

ISBN: 978-1-84717-046-0

4 6 8 10 9 7 5
14 16 18 17 15

Front cover photograph: Mark Monahan
Layout and design: The O'Brien Press Ltd
Printed and bound by Clondalkin Digital Print
The paper in this book is produced using pulp from managed forests

Every effort has been made to trace holders of copyright material; if any
infringement has inadvertently occured, the publishers ask the copyright holders
to contact them.

The O'Brien Press receives financial assistance from

Dedication

For my son, Jamie, with all my love.

Acknowledgements

I would like to thank everyone at The O'Brien Press, especially my editor, Helen Carr, Emma Byrne for the amazing book design, Mary Webb (Editorial Director) for believing in me and encouraging me to write this book, and Michael O'Brien (Publisher) for, yet again, supporting my writing ventures.

A huge thanks must go to Paul Faughnan of St Patrick's GAA Club, Palmerstown, for his technical help and advice with this book, and for all his brilliant answers to my endless GAA questions.

Thanks also to Donal Ryan of St Patrick's GAA Club, for his kind invitation to watch the kids of St Patrick's train, and to Marian Butler of WDAR 96fm for introducing me to St Patrick's GAA Club.

Thanks to Anita and Evan for their valued teenage input.

Many thanks to all the booksellers, librarians and everyone involved in the world of literature, who have supported me so kindly.

I would also like to acknowledge the countless hours of GAA footage that Setanta Sports and TG4 provided for me, in the comfort of my own sitting room, which assisted me in getting into a GAA frame of mind to write this book!

Finally, and most importantly, I would like to thank my wife, Mandy, for her support and encouragement, which make the world of difference, and my son, Jamie, for all the smiles, cuddles and games of football that make every day the best day.

Contents

Chapter 1

The Littlestown Crokes

'll be over in a minute!' shouted Danny Wilde, captain of the Littlestown Crokes under-13s, to his dad.

Danny's dad, Mick, was the coach of the GAA football team, which was named after Littlestown Lawns, the estate where Danny and Mick lived.

Mick Wilde had finally managed to gather all the other players in the dressing rooms, but Danny always had his own little routine before he joined his team mates for a home game. Just one moment alone, pitch side, to clear his head of absolutely everything except football and the match ahead.

Danny just loved home games. The smell of

the freshly-cut grass, along with the sight of the chalky straight lines that he and his dad had worked so hard on that morning, really got the butterflies going in his stomach.

Summer had passed so quickly and already September was nearing its end. It was over half-way through the season and it was the second league game since the June break-up. Danny's team had fought and battled their way to the top of the league, just one point ahead of the other title contenders, Barnfield GFC.

Only four more games after this one, and we could be league winners, thought Danny. Like a true captain, he was confident that his team could go all the way, but deep down inside, he knew that the final game on 8 November at home against Barnfield would be the under-13's Judgement Day.

Danny turned and took one more quick glance at the pitch that his dad called the 'Little Croker', then he swiftly headed for the dressing rooms to join his team mates for his dad's pre-match talk.

Danny's Jack Russell, Heffo, the team mascot, was sniffing around the door of the opposition's dressing room. He was kitted out in his all-blue custom-made jersey, and to look at him, one would think he was earwigging for any kind of opposition tactics that might help the home team.

Danny called him as he opened the dressing room door, and backed it up with a familiar two-tone whistle.

'About time!' complained Mick.

'Sorry, Dad. It was Heffo. He was heading into the other dressing room, again!'

All the other players burst out laughing.

'Go on, Heffo!' cheered Little John Watson. 'Here, Mr Wilde, is Heffo playing today?'

'He'd get his game before you would!' answered a voice down the back.

The banter was getting out of hand now and even Heffo was barking his brains out.

'Shut up, Doyler,' muttered Little John.

Suddenly Mick blew as hard as he could on his whistle, and everyone froze, except poor Heffo, who scampered down the back of the dressing room and hid behind Paddy Timmons' training bag.

'Can I speak now?' asked Mick.

'Come on lads, settle down,' said Jimmy Murphy, the assistant coach, just to give a little bit of back up, even though Mick Wilde never needed back up when it came to managing the team.

'I'm making two changes from the last game,' began Mick. The word 'change' was probably the most feared word that a coach could throw out in a dressing room before a match.

All the lads – even Danny, who never took his place for granted – shivered a little, and looked anywhere rather than at their coach, just in case it might influence him to leave them off the team. That is, if he hadn't already.

'Kevin,' continued Mick, 'you're coming in at left full.'

Mick could hear Anto Farrell huff, but he didn't say anything. He'd have a word with him on the way over to the pitch. Anto hadn't played well in the last two games and Kevin Kinsella was putting in extra efforts in training. Mick always thought that a coach should explain to a player why he was dropping him, in private, one to one.

'Now, the other change I'm making is …' Mick paused and glanced around the dressing room. Every single player in the room, except Anto and Kevin, waited in nervous anticipation to hear their name and join Anto on the bench.

It was almost like a scene from *X-FACTOR*!

Mick stared at Doyler for a few seconds, saying nothing.

Poor Doyler tried his best not to make eye contact with the coach. *I should have kept my big gob shut*, he thought. *He's going to drop me for slagging off Little Johnner.*

Mick switched his eyes over towards Barry Sweeney, their centre full forward.

'Nice one!' thought Doyler. 'Safe!'

'Barry,' said Mick. 'I want you to switch with Doyler today and go into centre half forward.'

Doyler perked up. Now he was trying his very best to make eye contact with the coach.

'Doyler, you're going to full forward today. Their centre full back is nearly as tall as our big Johnner. You might have a better chance with him in the air than Barry.'

'Nice one, thanks Coach' said Doyler.

'Thank me on the pitch with scores,' replied Mick, 'and by the way, if I hear you picking on Little Johnner again, *he'll* be the one wearing the number fourteen shirt.'

Jimmy, the assistant coach, grabbed hold of the zip of the kit bag and ripped it open.

'Right,' he said. 'You know your numbers. Let's get ready.'

Mick filled in his team card while all the lads dived into the kit bag in search of their jerseys. You could tell who was playing and who wasn't – the players who were starting were attacking the kit bag like a pack of wolves. The subs, on the other hand, were sitting back from the frenzy waiting until the end to pick up their jerseys. Anto Farrell wasn't used to this, but this time, just like the other subs, he sat still, in absolutely no hurry to collect his jersey.

Mick handed the team card to Jimmy.

'In your capable hands, Jimmy,' said Mick.

Jimmy nodded at Mick and gave him a *You can count on me* look.

Even though everyone knew that Jimmy was no Mick Wilde when it came to GAA, he had been Mick's assistant for a long time and had Mick's trust and admiration. As soon as Jimmy noticed the boys lacing up their boots he blew on his whistle to try and muffle the pre-match banter and buzz that was customary in a home team dressing room.

'Right lads,' said Mick, 'listen up.'

'Come on, lads, quiet down there,' added Jimmy.

It was time for Mick's final words of encouragement.

'Lads, I want you to get stuck in there from the whistle,' he began. 'Midfield, chase every loose ball,' he instructed as he glanced over to Danny and Sean Dempsey, 'and defence, get in good blocks. Remember the best way to block is to dive at their feet. And Doyler, if you can't shake that full back and turn and shoot, feed it back to Barry and give him a shot.'

There was a knock at the door. It was the referee.

'Right, home team!' said the referee.

'Okay lads, on your feet!' said Mick. Then he finished with the final familiar words before every home game, 'When you go out onto that pitch lads, where are you playing?' asked Mick.

'The Little Croker!' replied all the lads.

'And how do we play every game?' asked Mick.

'*Like the all-Ireland final!*' cheered the whole dressing room.

Then, with a clatter of studs, the team raced out like an army going into battle.

Chapter 2

The Match Against
St Agnes' Boys

Mick Wilde's boys, in all-blue, lined up against the boys in red and green from St Agnes' Boys. Each player, from Paddy Timmons at right corner full back to Danny in midfield, right up to Doyler in full forward, anxiously awaited the throw-in.

Mick tied Heffo's lead to his bag and began his routine pacing up and down the line, while Jimmy just stood with his arms folded looking relaxed.

'Here we go,' announced Jimmy.

'Come on the Crokes!' shouted Mick.

'Ready, lads?' asked the ref.

Then he gave Danny and the St Agnes'

midfielder a nod. Danny and his opposite number raised their heads as the referee blew on his whistle and threw the ball high above them.

Danny was first in the air stretching his left hand above his opponent's. He passed the ball down to Sean Dempsey, then turned his man and headed for goal, leaving the St Agnes' number nine dazed with Danny's pace. The battle had commenced!

Dempsey kicked straight up to Barry Sweeney in centre half forward, who knocked a perfect pass out to Splinter Murphy.

Splinter threw a shimmy around his man and spotted Danny running in behind the full forward line.

Danny raised his hand.

Doyler made a run wide and opened up a gap for Danny.

Splinter knocked a sweet pass in towards Danny, who caught it beautifully on the run.

Danny took a quick glance at goal and

dropped the ball onto the side of his right boot.

The ball swerved past their keeper and into the top right corner.

GOAL!

'Come on, lads!' shouted Danny as he fisted the air in glorious celebration.

Mick and Jimmy were hopping around on the side line.

'What a dream start!' cheered Jimmy.

'Come on lads, settle down and back into it!' warned Mick.

Jimmy was right – Danny had given Littlestown Crokes the perfect dream start and it totally rattled the St Agnes' boys.

Barry Sweeney caught the kick out and knocked a long, high ball over for a point.

Crokes kept the ball in St Agnes' end of the field for the next twenty minutes, scoring four more points. Danny was playing a stormer in midfield, winning everything in the air and when they tried to break through, Danny relentlessly pulled off tackle after tackle.

When the ref blew for half time the Crokes were winning 1-5 to nil.

Poor Heffo jumped around on his toes like a ballerina as the fifteen thirsty warriors raided the bag for their half-time feast of oranges.

Mick let the boys have a few bites of their oranges before he started to talk.

'Right lads, gather around – Timmons don't give the dog orange. Well done lads, super, well done,' congratulated Mick. 'That was a dream start! Lovely goal, Danny. You kept the pressure on and didn't get slack, lads. That's exactly what was needed. They're putty in your hands out there. They don't know how to cope with yiz at all!'

Mick was in his stride when the ref blew his whistle for the second half.

'Okay lads, just keep it going. Don't nod off. It's nowhere near over. Keep the pressure on and the scores coming.'

'No changes, Mick?' asked Jimmy.

'Not at all, Jimmy,' confirmed Mick.

Mick wasn't sure whether Jimmy actually would have considered making a change while they were winning so easily, or whether he was just being kind to the subs by making the suggestion heard. Either way, thanks be to the gods of GAA that Mick never had to leave a match in an emergency and leave the reins to Jimmy. *God forbid!* thought Mick.

Once again Danny was in there like a dog after a bone, winning the throw in and knocking it back to Dempsey. But Dempsey obviously hadn't listened to Mick's half-time words, and now he was too busy looking over at Heffo, who was doing what looked like a breakdance manoeuvre to free his lead from the bag.

'Dempsey!' shouted Danny.

Dempsey was mortified and furious with himself. His man had gone on a solo and left him for dust. But Sean Dempsey wasn't nick-named 'Dirty Dempsey' for no reason – he tracked the ball and when it came to the St

Agnes' centre half forward and he had cleverly turned Alan Whelan, Crokes' centre half back, Dirty Dempsey went in for the killer tackle.

CRUNCH!

The poor centre half forward didn't know what hit him. Dempsey hurtled into him, taking him and the ball through the air.

The St Agnes' players all circled around Dempsey, while their injured player rolled around the ground – he was so convincing that he could probably have given the Portuguese soccer team a few tips!

The referee blew furiously on his whistle and Mick rushed over with some water and a can of Deep Heat; he was genuinely worried about the young lad, but he also wanted to make peace with his opposite coach.

The shaken centre half forward finally hobbled to his feet and once the ref could see that calm was restored he charged and sentenced Dirty Dempsey with one swift wave of the red card.

'You're off your head!' roared a disputing voice from the home team's line.

It was Dempsey's dad, Tommy.

'Keep him quiet,' the ref warned Mick, who was seizing the opportunity to instruct Barry Sweeney to drop back to midfield with Danny.

Mick glanced over at Tommy with a *Keep your mouth shut or else!* look. Tommy Dempsey was nothing but an interfering, loud-mouthed, know-it-all who was itching to be the team coach. He and Mick had had many run-ins in training and at matches and Mick was starting to run out of patience with him.

'That should have been a yellow!' yelled Tommy.

'It was a straight red,' replied Mick, and jogged back to his coaching position alongside poor Jimmy who was as quiet as a mouse. Jimmy was a big softy who would absolutely never under any circumstances get into a fight, not even to help Mick fend off a big eejit like Tommy Dempsey.

The ref blew his whistle and while Mick and Tommy Dempsey exchanged heated debates on the line, the number nine for St Agnes' kicked the ball nicely into his centre full forward who had run in behind a distracted Big Johnner, Crokes' centre full back. Liam Darcy, Crokes' goalkeeper had come out to cover Big Johnner, but the cheeky number fourteen fisted the perfect pass over his head and in for a goal!

The first Mick knew about it was when he saw the opposite line jumping in celebration.

'Did they score, Jimmy?' asked Mick.

'A goal!' answered Jimmy with his hands on his head. 'Big Johnner was busy watching you two go mad at it.'

Mick was furious with himself. He knew that it was his job to keep situations under control and there he was involved in a stupid row instead of organising his players.

'Right lads, don't let it get to yiz,' encouraged Mick. 'Pick it up again!'

But it did get to them as, straight from the

kick out, St Agnes' won the ball and it was fed out to their right full forward who drilled it high and over for a brilliant point. They were on the comeback and in the next ten minutes they wouldn't let Danny's team get the ball out of their half and managed to put two more points over the bar.

There were ten minutes left to play and the score was narrowed down to 1-5 to 1-3 for Danny's team.

Danny knew that he had to knuckle in and take the game by the scruff of the neck.

He dropped a little deeper into defence alongside his centre half back as he knew that was more or less the range of his keeper.

Darcy, the goal keeper, spotted Danny hovering to the side of Alan Whelan and he aimed his kick out towards him.

As soon as the ball came into range, Danny jumped into its flight path and made a cracking catch. Then he turned like a gazelle on the run from a lion and went on a Danny Wilde solo.

'Go on, Danny!' shouted Mick.

'Go on, skin them Danny!' seconded Jimmy.

Danny's team mates advanced forward, but watched as Danny magnificently fended off two tackles and powered ahead into St Agnes' centre half back line.

He threw a dummy effort to pass to Splinter who had moved over to support him and then fisted a pass to Doyler, the centre full forward.

The next move was a move that Mick had his forward line practise strenuously: Doyler made absolutely no attempt to catch the pass, he fisted the ball over his marker's head and back into the path of Danny.

Then Danny took a chance and instead of letting the ball bounce in front of him as practised, he snapped a shot on the volley and hit a screamer into the back of the net!

Danny had pulled off a ridiculously amazing score that no amount of practice could teach or train you to perfect – it was just pure talent!

Danny's goal had lifted Crokes' heads again

and St Agnes' Boys once again fell apart, and no matter how much they tried to get back up-field for scores, the Crokes' defence gelled together and broke them down with ease.

The referee looked at his watch one last time and blew the full time whistle.

Danny's team had beaten St Agnes' Boys by 2-5 to 1-3.

Mick patted Jimmy on the back, and then as usual, let the team mascot off his lead.

Heffo raced onto the pitch and while the Crokes' players all congratulated each other and commiserated with their deflated opponents, Heffo put nose to ball and went off on a doggy solo, turning and twisting in circles until he was so tired he collapsed and rolled over on his back on the dry grass.

Mick paced over to the other coach and shook his hand.

'Hard luck. Good game,' said Mick, politely.

As soon as Mick turned away, a man in a sports jacket with a newspaper tucked under his arm approached him.

'Good win,' said the man.

Mick didn't know him, but he thought his face looked a little familiar.

'Thanks. We lost concentration for a bit, but they're good lads. They pulled it back.'

Mick wasn't stopping for a chat, but the stranger put his arm out to suggest a conversation.

'Eh! I have to say, your number nine has real talent.'

'Yeah, Danny's a good player. He's my son.'

'You must be proud as punch,' chuckled the man.

The man pulled out his ID card and flashed it at Mick.

'Sorry, Mick, is it? Excuse my manners. Robert Jenkins is my name. I'm a representative for the Dublin schoolboys' development squad.'

Mick instantly raised an eyebrow and perked up like a soldier on parade.

A scout!

That's it, he thought. *I knew I'd seen his face before. He's been at a couple of other games, lurking in the background with his newspaper, like a spy in action.*

'I have to say I'm very impressed with Danny. I heard about him through the grapevine. I hope you don't mind, but I've watched a few of your games and I think your son has the ability to play at higher levels.'

'Oh, yeah? Well, I wouldn't argue with you on that one,' agreed Mick calmly, but behind his calm exterior his stomach was in knots. He knew what was coming next.

'We meet about six times a year to get a good look at up and coming talent like Danny. Is there any chance that Danny could come for a training session with our squad next Friday?' asked Mr Jenkins.

'Absolutely!' said Mick, grinning from ear to ear.

The scout, as Mick called him, gave Mick a

card with the address of the training grounds and his number on it, and shook hands with the proud father.

'If there's any problem or anything at all, just give me a bell.'

Then he tucked his newspaper back under his arm and headed briskly off across the fields into the distance, leaving Mick standing smiling and holding the card tight like it was a winning lotto ticket.

Chapter 3

Granny Maureen's Birthday

As always, reliable Jimmy took down the nets while Mick followed the boys into the dressing rooms to congratulate them and have his post-match chat.

Sean 'Dirty' Dempsey and his dad weren't in the dressing rooms. They had gone off home sulking before the match had even finished.

Mick was itching to tell Danny about his trial with the Dublin team, but he thought it would be better if he didn't say anything in the dressing room.

I'll tell him on his own first, thought Mick, *and sure he can tell the other lads himself.*

Mick, Danny, Jimmy and his son Splinter,

their left full forward, carried the gear and balls home, as they only lived around the corner from the playing fields.

'Danny, are you coming over for a game on my PlayStation?' asked Splinter who had just got a new game for his birthday.

'Nah! I can't, Splinter,' replied Danny. 'It's my granny's birthday and we're going straight over there to see her.'

'Thanks Jimmy, I'll see you on Tuesday night,' said Mick. 'I'll see you, Damien,' he said to Splinter. 'You played a great game!'

'Can we bring Heffo to Granny's?' asked Danny.

'I suppose so. Tie him to the gate and I'll bring in the bags. Then you run in and wash your face for Granny.'

Mick and Danny set off to visit Mick's mother, Maureen, who only lived a ten-minute walk away in an old folks' complex of flats called 'Shady Cedars'.

During the walk, Mick broke the good

news to Danny.

'Are you for real, Dad?' asked Danny.

'Yep! Next Friday evening, you're going to be training with the Dublin development team, son. It will be the proudest moment of my life, Danny,' said Mick with unexpected emotion.

'Savage!' said Danny. 'Mammy would be chuffed. Wouldn't she, Dad?'

'Your mother will be shining down on you, Danny, like she does at all of your games.'

Danny's mam had passed away when Danny was just a baby, but Mick always tried to keep her very much in Danny's life by talking to Danny about her as much as possible.

'Come on, Dad, we'll run the rest of the way. I can't wait to tell Granny,' said Danny excitedly.

Danny and Heffo raced ahead of Mick, but almost immediately Danny came walking back around the corner towards Mick, who had pulled up for a breather.

'I'm all right, son. Just give us a second!'

gasped Mick. 'You're too fast for me.'

'Dad, you're not going to like what you're going to see when you turn the corner,' warned Danny.

'Not the Bentley!' said Mick. He sounded gutted.

'Yep!'

Mick and Danny had been trying to get to Granny's early to avoid meeting Danny's rich and snobby Uncle Larry, Mick's brother.

The only time that the brothers crossed paths was on their mother's birthday and Mick didn't want a repeat of last year's row. Mick and Larry despised each other.

'We'll come back later,' said Mick.

'Ah, Da!' moaned Danny. 'I'm dying to tell Granny my good news.'

Good news! thought Mick. *That's right. I'll relish the look on Larry's face when he hears about Danny's trial.*

'You're right, son,' said Mick. 'Why should we back down?'

Mick let Heffo off his lead at the gates and he instantly ran over to Larry's Bentley and cocked his leg.

Mick was thrilled because he knew that all Larry ever did during his one and only annual visit to their mother was stand at her window and watch his precious car.

'Come on, Heffo!' called Danny as he rang his granny's door bell.

'He's all right, son,' grinned Mick. 'Better on your uncle's wheels than on Granny's floor!'

Danny laughed with his dad.

The front door was opened by Larry's wife, Regina.

'Michael, darling!' screeched Regina. 'And Daniel! Oh, you've grown *so* tall since last year!'

Danny smiled politely at his aunt and quickly brushed past her into the house. He only met Regina once a year, but once a year was enough for him to come to the conclusion that she was away with the fairies.

'Regina,' acknowledged Mick.

Danny ran over to Granny Maureen and gave her a big hug. She was in her new, leather, multi-functional reclining chair that Larry had had delivered for her birthday.

Larry made an effort to turn away from the curtains just to see the look on poor Mick's face when he saw his mother's present.

'Nice chair!' said Danny.

'It's very cosy,' answered Granny, 'but I don't know about all these buttons. It's like sitting in a space ship.'

Mick laughed.

'You want to watch yourself, Mam. We don't want you taking off now, do we?'

'Did you tell your granny your news, son?' asked Mick.

Danny announced his good news to all. His cousins – Jonathon who was twelve like Danny and Lowry who was fourteen – came in from the kitchen to politely congratulate him. Regina didn't really want to be there and she certainly didn't want her children there, but she always – especially in public – insisted on good manners, politeness and smiles.

'The cake!' said Granny after she'd praised Danny. 'Are we going to cut the cake?'

'In a jiffy,' said Regina and she rushed out to the kitchen and quickly came back in with a delicious fresh cream chocolate gateau.

When Regina asked who wanted a slice of cake, everyone put their hand up, even Larry. The atmosphere was brutal and everyone knew that if they were busy eating cake then they wouldn't have to make any effort to strike up stupid, pointless conversation.

'Danny,' said Mick while licking the last of his cream from his fork. 'Get your ball out from the cupboard and bring Jonathon outside for a kickabout.'

Danny jumped up.

'Are you on, Jonathon?'

Before Jonathon even considered answering he glanced over at his dad.

Larry said nothing, but his facial expression said clearly, *No way, young man*!

'Ah come on, Larry,' said Mick.

Regina became very twitchy in her seat, wondering if a repeat of last year's episode between the two brothers was going to start off again.

She decided to take control.

'Darling, Jonathon, just go out for a few minutes with Daniel. We'll be leaving shortly.'

'Why don't you go and play too, Lowry,' suggested Granny with more cake in her mouth than teeth.

Lowry panicked.

'I don't think so, Gran. I just got a new pair of shoes.'

Granny looked down to check.

'Oh! They're lovely. Did you get them in Dunnes Stores? Yes! I'm sure I saw them in Dunnes.'

Jonathon laughed as he and Danny were going out the door.

Lowry couldn't keep up the polite game.

Granny had gone *too* far with that comment and the thought of Jonathon repeating it to any of her friends made her heave.

'Oh my God! Granny! These are Nine West!'

Outside, Danny was telling Jonathon more about his trial with the Dublin team.

'Here, catch!' said Danny and he fisted the ball to his cousin.

Jonathon caught the ball and just stood there with it.

'Kick it back!' said Danny.

Jonathon looked around to check if his dad was watching.

Danny noticed his cousin's reluctance to be seen participating.

'Why won't your dad let you play football?' asked Danny.

This conversation was leading him into unfamiliar territory. Danny didn't know any-body who wouldn't be allowed to play football.

Jonathon was a little embarrassed now, so he copied Danny's pass and fisted the ball back to him.

'Nice pass! Would you *like* to play football?' asked Danny.

'I suppose so,' answered Jonathon. 'I've never had the opportunity, so I'm not sure if I'd like it or not.'

'Are you mad?' argued Danny. 'You'd love it. It's great fun. A real buzz!'

'Really?' Jonathon was beginning to like the sound of it.

Just as the two boys were beginning to enjoy the game, the Bentley bleeped three times and Larry barged out of the flat.

'Into the car, Jonathon!' ordered Larry.

Regina followed him, with Lowry trailing behind.

'Laurence!' screeched Regina. 'You *can't* leave on these terms.'

Danny and Jonathon looked at each other, and without saying anything each cousin knew what the other was thinking. Their dads had just had their annual disagreement.

'Come on in, Danny,' said Mick as the Bentley disappeared down the road.

'What happened?' asked Danny. He was a bit annoyed; he was actually enjoying talking to his cousin.

'Your daddy and your uncle,' answered Granny. 'That's what happened. I'm sick to death of yiz at each other's throats. For heavens sake, I'd wish yiz would just bury the hatchet and try to move on.'

'Right, Mam! We're off. Happy birthday. I love you!' said Mick as he grabbed his coat with unusual urgency.

'What's Granny on about?' asked Danny.

'Just give your granny a hug and a kiss, son,' insisted Mick, and he nodded a look to Danny as if to say, *And mind your own business as well.*

Chapter 4

The Kerryman

On Monday morning in Irish class Danny was telling Splinter how excited he was about his trial on Friday and that he felt sorry for his cousin Jonathon who wasn't even allowed to play football.

'What colour is your uncle's Bentley?' asked Splinter, who was car-mad. 'Is it a soft top? Marky Byrne saw a soft top one in town last week. They're dead rare!' babbled Splinter.

Just as Danny was about to answer, Mr O'Shea stopped reading.

Danny and Splinter looked up to see Mr O'Shea staring down at them.

'Would Mr Wilde and Mr Murphy care to share with us *exactly* what is so important that you have to discuss it while I'm reading?'

Danny and Splinter buried their heads in their books. They weren't even on the right page.

'Stand up, boys,' ordered Mr O'Shea.

As Danny stood up, the teacher asked the question again – he wasn't about to let it go.

'Em, football, sir,' answered Danny. 'Gaelic football.'

This was a clever move by Danny; he knew that Mr O'Shea was a passionate GAA supporter. Sure it would be a county crime if he wasn't as he hailed from 'The Kingdom' itself!

'GAA you say, Danny.'

This was a good sign, he had addressed Danny by his first name.

Danny quickly elaborated on his answer.

'Yes, sir! We were just talking about how Kerry has won the most All-Ireland Finals.'

Mr O'Shea smiled. He was onto Danny, but he admired the boy's ingenuity and also enjoyed the fact that all the other boys were now looking at Danny and wondering why he was talking about Kerry and not the Dubs.

'Is that right, Wilde?'

Bad sign! thought Danny. *O'Shea's reverted back to surnames.*

'So tell me, Wilde. Do you know how many times Kerry has won the All- Ireland, then?'

Splinter leaned his right leg against his desk, just enough to discreetly rest a sufficient amount of body weight on it without being accused of slumping. Splinter, along with Danny and every other pupil in the class, knew what was coming. Mr O'Shea was about to kick into 'Kerry Mode', and they were probably in for a long speech about how wonderful the 'Kingdom' was and how Kerry was the best GAA team.

Danny thought he had worked out the right answer.

'Em! I think it's about twenty-five times, sir.'

'Wrong, Wilde, by a long shot!' Mr O'Shea

was chuffed. He had a smile now on his face that Danny recognised – the same smile that Danny had seen on the faces of forty thousand Kerry men, women and children in Croke Park, the day he witnessed Kerry knock the Dubs out of the All-Ireland semis.

'Thirty-five times the magnificent Sam has travelled down to the Kingdom!' answered Mr O'Shea. 'And do you know how many times Kerry has beaten the Dubs?' continued Mr O'Shea. He was on a roll now; he could almost feel the insults that every pupil in the class was hurling at him in their minds. He didn't care. He was enjoying the moment.

Danny decided that enough was enough. This was battle, just like on the playing field and he was going to hit back with a score of his own, a big score.

'Em! I'm not too sure about that one either, Sir, but I can tell you one time when the Dubs beat Kerry.'

'Is that right, Wilde? *One* time the Dubs

beat Kerry!' Mr O'Shea chuckled.

'Yeah, Sir! It was the best game of football ever. The '77 semi-final. And the Dubs won it!'

'That's right, Wilde.'

Mr O'Shea wasn't smiling anymore. Danny had tugged on the one thorn that stuck deep in the side of every Kerry supporter. The '77 semi. It was the greatest contest of football ever played in the land, and Danny Wilde knew it, and had just announced it to everyone else in the class.

'You're a bit young to know about that match, Wilde,' quizzed Mr O'Shea.

'It's his favourite, Sir,' intervened Splinter who was now half-sitting on his desk. 'He even named his dog "Heffo" after the Dubs' man-ager.'

'Straighten up, Murphy!' yelled Mr O'Shea.

That was the end of all GAA talk. Mr O'Shea picked up reading where he had left off, just to show Danny that although he acknowledged that score – that very big score – he would have the last say.

The two boys remained standing for the rest of Irish class, which was almost like Chinese torture. It was hard enough to try and stay awake in Irish class sitting down without the burden of having to stand through it.

On the way home from school, Danny and Splinter swapped compliments on how the other had stood up to the teacher and put him in his place.

'Ah! But you topped it off Danny, bringing up the '77 semi!'

'Yeah!' smirked Danny. 'My da always said ...' and Splinter joined in, '... *If you're ever in a battle of GAA talk with a Kerry supporter, just mention the '77 semi.*'

*   *   *

Later that evening, Danny told Mick all about that day's Irish class.

'Don't be winding up your teachers, son,' advised Mick.

'But Dad! I couldn't help it. He kept going on

about Kerry this and Kerry that and then he started picking on the Dubs.'

'Did you mention the '77 semi?' asked Mick with great anticipation of the answer.

'I did!' Danny answered with pride bursting from the seams.

'I bet he went all quiet,' said Mick.

'Not another word, Da!'

Mick was in great humour now, and he decided that they should order a curry to celebrate Danny's trial with the Dublin team, and just to top the evening off, he dug out the '77 semi video.

When the doorbell rang, Danny answered the door. It was their curry arriving.

'How much do we owe him, son?' asked Mick.

'Nine eighty,' answered the curry man.

'I'll be back in a second,' said Danny.

When Danny returned with the money, the curry man was stretching his head as far around the door as possible to catch a glimpse of the match. He jumped back when Danny came running out.

'Eh, that wouldn't be the '77 All-Ireland semi between the Dubs and Kerry, would it?'

'It would indeed!' Mick yelled out. 'Do you want to watch a bit of it?'

Almost as soon as the words had left Mick's lips, the curry man was on the couch, dipping the very chips he'd just delivered into poor Danny's rapidly-declining tub of sauce, and howling, 'Up the Dubs!' at the telly.

Danny, his dad and the curry man rode an emotional rollercoaster as they watched the Kerrymen charge at the Dubs and, in rapid response, the Dubs counterattack the boys from the Kingdom. The ultimate Dublin piece of warrior showmanship came when Dubs' defender, Sean Doherty, plucked a long Kerry free kick out of the air and harm's way and sent it up field.

The three sofa spectators watched in awe as the Dubs battled and grinded the ball out of the chaotic midfield up to the hands of Tony Hanahoe, who passed it to Bernard Brogan, who charged towards the Kerry goal and then unleashed a thundering shot that saw the ball rip past the Kerry goalkeeper and smash into the now fragile and battered netting.

Danny, his dad and the curry man leapt off the sofa and celebrated as if they had travelled back in time and were amongst all the fans in Hill 16.

Danny fell asleep that night thinking about the legends of GAA history and dreaming that by Friday evening he could be taking his first steps to becoming a Dublin legend himself.

Chapter 5

A Dirty Player

As if nothing had happened on Saturday, Sean Dempsey and his trouble-making dad, Tommy, turned up for training on Tuesday evening.

Mick wasn't really in the humour for more conflict so he just let Sean participate in training and he kept his distance from Tommy, who was unusually quiet, watching the session from behind one of the goal posts.

Mick ran the boys through their normal routine, starting them with a few warm-up exercises with Jimmy and then a couple of laps around the full length of the pitch while he set out the cones at the edge of the playing fields to benefit from the street lamps.

'Right! Bring them in, Jimmy,' yelled Mick, and everyone gathered around their coach, slightly red-faced and gasping for breath.

'Well done, lads. Thanks, Jimmy,' said Mick.

Danny and his team-mates did fifteen minutes of different exercise techniques, from sprint racing in and out of the cones to dribbling the ball to passing the ball from one end to the other and then sprinting to the other end.

Training for Littlestown Crokes was hard, but it kept Danny and the other players superfit and that had a lot to do with why they were top of their league.

Mick always liked to finish training with a short friendly match between the players just to keep the morale up. *All training and no play doesn't make good team players,* thought Mick.

Jimmy and a few of the players set up a small pitch with the cones. Mick split the players into two sides; he would be referee.

Training matches were always a mixture of competitiveness and fun, and that's exactly how this game was going until one stupid tackle changed the whole enjoyable atmosphere completely.

There were only a couple of minutes of training left when Danny pulled off the perfect pick-up and went on a galloping solo down the line. He threw a dummy and swerved around Paddy Timmons, then he hand-passed to Splinter who repeated the skill over Little Johnner Watson's head, sending the ball back into the hands of Danny.

Danny now had the goal within range. He released the ball from his right hand into the path of his dynamic right foot.

Then, BANG! Just as Danny was about to strike, Dempsey, who had been following his every move, took his legs from under him.

This was a foul that Dirty Dempsey had been warned about many a time, but this time he was in big trouble. This was the last straw – in Mick

Wilde's book taking out a team mate in training was scraping the bottom of the barrel.

Danny rolled around the ground in agonising pain, while Mick blew hard on his whistle until he had no more breath left in him to push out his anger at Dempsey.

Dempsey stepped back while Jimmy held Danny and Mick examined his right leg.

'Is it broken, Mick?' asked Jimmy with his head slightly turned away as he was quite squeamish.

'I don't think so,' answered Mick.

Danny had already calmed down and that was a good sign.

'Can you stand, son?' asked Mick.

'I think so, Dad,' replied Danny, but it was obvious he was still in a lot of discomfort.

Everybody was relieved to see Danny back on his feet, and none more so than the captain himself – he *had* to be fit for the trial on Friday!

'Right! We'll leave it at that, lads!' announced Mick. 'Damien, could you help Danny home?

I've business to take care of. I'll follow on.'

Sean Dempsey was walking over to his dad when Mick caught up with him.

'Sean!' called Mick.

Dempsey hesitantly turned around and his dad, Tommy, followed him over to Mick.

'That was out of order,' said Mick.

Tommy Dempsey was about to say something, no doubt in his son's defence, but Mick didn't give him a chance. He was determined this time to finish what he had started.

'Let me finish,' said Mick, pointing to Dempsey's dad with fierce authority. 'You're a decent player, Sean,' started Mick, 'but you're out of control.'

Mick looked at Tommy, as if to partially blame him for that.

Sean didn't open his mouth, and he didn't show any remorse either.

'I've given you chance after chance, but that's it, Sean, you're off the team – for good. You can go and join some other club and torture their coach with your vicious antics.'

'You can't kick him off the team!' argued Tommy.

'I just did and I'm not going to change my mind. You'd want to stop sticking up for your son when he does bad things, Tommy, and start encouraging him to improve his social behaviour.'

If there was one thing Tommy Dempsey loathed it was being told what to do.

Tommy grabbed Sean by the sleeve of his shirt and dragged him off, but he'd only managed a dozen strides or so before he pulled up.

'You can stick your team, Wilde. I'm going to get him on a decent team next season,' Tommy called back. 'One with a proper manager too. Maybe Barnfield.'

'You do that, Tommy,' answered Mick. He was relieved to see the back of the two of them as they disappeared across the fields and quickly became a couple of dots and finally just a bad memory.

Mick put plenty of ice on Danny's leg when he got home and told him that he could take the next couple of days off school to rest it.

Mick was just as worried as Danny about the trial on Friday and equally unsure whether Danny's leg would be well enough in time.

Danny spent most of Wednesday on the sofa with his leg up on two pillows and covered with an ice pack. Normally he'd be chuffed to bits about having a couple of days off school, but this time was different. This time getting better quick was a priority to Danny.

Danny played his GAA dvds all day trying to pick up tips and moves for Friday just in case he was fit enough for his trial.

Splinter knocked over to see him after school and schemed with Danny to bunk off school the next day.

'Wait until you see my dad driving off to work, Splinter,' said Danny, 'then come around to the house.'

'Nice one, Danny,' smiled Splinter. 'It'll be animal not going to school.'

Chapter 6

A Day Off School

The next morning, after Mick had driven off to work, Danny texted Splinter that the coast was clear. Splinter had been hiding around the corner under a big Leyland hedge.

The morning flew in with Splinter to keep him company and Danny's leg felt almost better. All the sitting around with ice had done the trick!

The two pals were stuck into a game on Splinter's PlayStation when the doorbell rang.

Splinter jumped up.

'Who's that?'

Poor Splinter had never bunked off school before and was now terrified that he would be caught.

Danny peeped out through the curtains as the door bell rang and rang and rang.

'It's my granny!' said Danny.

Splinter was relieved.

'Just hide until she goes. Don't let her in, Danny!'

'I have to let her in, Splinter! She's not budging and she'll tell my da that I didn't answer.'

'What am I going to do?' Splinter started to panic.

'Hide under the stairs,' said Danny. 'She won't stay long.'

And so Splinter hid under the stairs, as deep in as he could behind some coats.

Danny opened the door for his granny and held his right leg up off the floor and balanced on his left one to convince his granny that he had had to struggle to the door. It worked.

'You poor chicken-hen,' sympathised Granny Maureen. 'I've brought you around a bowl of lovely stew – that will help put a spring back in your step. You sit back down there, pet, and I'll re-heat it for you.'

'Thanks, Granny,' smiled Danny as he spotted Splinter peeping out through the door under the stairs.

'I'll just take my coat off. Sure I might as well stay for a while and keep you company.'

Splinter leapt back and fell over the hoover.

'What was that?' Granny got an awful fright.

'Nothing, Granny,' said Danny.

'What do you mean?' asked Granny. 'Something moved or fell or some sort of noise came from under that stairs.'

She was getting stressed now.

Danny had to act quick as he knew well that Granny Maureen was as bad as a pit bull terrier when it came to letting go of something.

'Sorry, Granny. It's my training bag. The hook on the wall keeps falling off.'

Granny threw her coat on the arm of the sofa.

'You'd want to get your daddy to fix it properly. Mother of Divine Jerusalem, frights like that would be the death of your poor oul' grandmother!'

Then she went out to the kitchen to stick the bowl of stew in the microwave.

If Splinter thought that his visit in under the stairs was going to be a quick one, then he was wrong. It was more like doing solitary confinement. Once Danny's granny sat down she had no intentions of moving for a long spell.

Danny felt sorry for Splinter. *I wonder if he can breathe in there?* he thought after an hour and a half had passed. Danny had even put on a GAA match to try and get Granny moving, but she watched it all, and was half way through her second match with Danny.

'You know, Danny …' said Granny, out of the blue.

Danny jumped in anticipation. Was this the moment? Was she actually going?

'Yes, Gran?'

'Your daddy was a great footballer.'

'So he tells me, Granny,' replied Danny, slumping back down into the sofa.

'He loved his football. Him and your uncle Larry.'

Danny perked up again.

'Larry? Larry played GAA?' Danny was gobsmacked. Granny must be confused or maybe thinking of one of Mick's friends or something like that. *There's no way Uncle Larry played GAA*, Danny thought.

'Oh, yes!' said Granny with great assurance in her voice. 'My two boys *loved* their football, until …'

Granny stopped in her tracks.

Danny sat up with his jaw hanging open, waiting for the rest of Granny's sentence, but nothing came out. She just stared at the telly, clicking her bottom set of false teeth in and out of her mouth, as if they hadn't even been having a conversation.

Finally Danny's curiosity got the better of him.

'Until *what*, Gran?' Danny asked.

Splinter who had been on the verge of

nodding off, was back at the slightly ajar door, only this time it was his left ear that was peeping out.

Granny jumped up.

'Is that the time? Holy Mary! I'd best be getting off.'

'Ah! Tell us Granny!' pleaded Danny.

Splinter had to put his hand over his mouth as he nearly spurted out a back-up plea.

Granny sat back down.

'I shouldn't be dragging up the past, Danny. Your daddy wouldn't like me to say anything.'

Dad! thought Danny. *What's the big secret with Dad?*

Danny thought he and his dad had no secrets. He thought that they were rock solid since his mam died. He was even more determined now than before to find out more.

'I won't say a word, Granny. Honestly!'

'All right, pet! Did you ever wonder why your daddy and your uncle never got on? Why they're always at each others' throats when they see each other?'

'Yeah!' answered Danny. His dad had explained things to him before. 'Dad told me that they just grew apart over the years until they didn't really have anything in common anymore.'

Granny bowed her head.

That wasn't exactly the whole story.

Danny's granny went on to tell him all about how his dad and his uncle Larry were once very, very good GAA players.

'Your daddy was probably a little bit better than your uncle,' she explained, 'but your Uncle Larry was very bright, a bit of an academic, and he was offered a scholarship to study and also play GAA. The two lads always got on well, but your uncle used to tease your daddy about not being as good at school.'

She paused.

'Then it happened,' she said.

'What happened?' asked Danny.

'The injury,' said Granny. 'And the fight.'

Splinter was *so* delighted that he'd bunked off school. Being stuck in solitary confinement under the stairs with hot gossip like this was savage.

Granny told Danny how the day after Larry announced his big news, he broke his hand in two places from a tackle made by Danny's dad, Mick, in a kickabout on the road.

Danny couldn't believe what he was hearing. Mick Wilde *despised* dirty tackles and foul play.

'It must have been an accident!' Danny defended his dad.

'That's what your daddy said, and to this day, Danny, I believe him!' said Granny, 'but your Uncle Larry's hand never healed properly and he missed out on his scholarship. He and your daddy had a huge row and your uncle wouldn't believe that it was an accident. Larry was *convinced* that your daddy was jealous and he intended to injure him.'

Poor Danny. This was all too hard for him, and although he was convinced that his dad would never deliberately have set out to ruin Larry's hopes, he couldn't stop the little haunting doubts that were nibbling away at him.

Finally, Granny went home, but before she left, she made Danny swear on the Holy Bible that he wouldn't ever breathe a word of their conversation to his dad.

Splinter's legs were killing him when he finally got out from under the stairs.

'No wonder your uncle doesn't like your da!' said Splinter as he tried to stretch out every crease and knot in his muscles.

'Splinter!' said Danny in a grown-up tone. 'Don't repeat *any* of that to *anyone*. There's no way my da did that on purpose. No way!' insisted Danny.

'No he didn't, Danny,' agreed Splinter. 'Your da is sound.'

'Promise me, Splinter, you won't say anything.'

'Water off a duck's back!' said Splinter, and he and Danny set up the PlayStation game again until it was time for Splinter to head off home.

Chapter 7

Disaster!

Even though Danny was dying to question his dad about the incident with Uncle Larry, he had sworn to Granny not to breathe a word.

Mick noticed Danny was extra-quiet at dinner.

'You're very quiet, son,' quizzed Mick. 'Are you worried about your trial?'

'Well, a little bit.'

'You'll be fine, son. Your leg should be as good as new by tomorrow. I'll tell you what – if you don't think you're up to it tomorrow, I'll dig out that card and ring Mr Jenkins and explain everything. He'll be sound, son. He'll probably reschedule. How's that, Danny?'

'Animal, Da!' answered Danny, but the trial wasn't on his mind. He just couldn't get Granny's story out of his head.

Mick had persuaded Danny to stay at home and not even bother to go and watch training that night. *The more rest the better*, thought Mick.

Danny didn't mind. Actually he preferred to stay at home, as being a spectator at training or at matches was frustrating and he would only be itching to get involved.

Mick was only gone about half an hour when the doorbell rang.

I wonder who that is? thought Danny. *Maybe Da forgot something.*

Danny opened the door and there was Jimmy, panting like mad.

'What's up, Jimmy?' Danny was getting worried. Jimmy had that familiar 'Jimmy look' on him that he got when something was wrong.

'Get your coat, Danny,' instructed Jimmy.

Danny had never heard Jimmy give an order with such urgency.

'Why?' he asked

Jimmy paused, then said, 'It's your daddy, Danny.'

'What's happened to my dad?'

'I don't know, Danny. He just collapsed.'

'Is he all right, Jimmy? Is he all right?' Danny was almost crying now. His dad was his whole world.

'I think so, Danny. He's gone off in an ambulance.' Jimmy didn't sound very convincing.

Danny ran in, completely forgetting about his sore leg, and grabbed his jacket. Jimmy had his car already ticking over outside.

'What about my granny?' asked Danny as they drove by Shady Cedars.

Poor Jimmy was sweating – this was just too much for him.

'We better not tell your granny yet, Danny. Don't want to frighten her now do we?'

Jimmy's words reminded Danny of Granny's fright earlier that day.

'No, sure my dad can ring her later, Jimmy, can't he?'

'Good man, Danny. Of course he can.'

When Danny and Jimmy arrived at the hospital, they were told that Mick was unconscious and the doctors were carrying out tests, and to expect a long wait before any news.

'Why is he having tests?' Danny kept hounding Jimmy for answers.

Eventually poor Jimmy couldn't handle any more.

'I think we should give your granny a ring,' he suggested.

'I thought we didn't want to frighten her?' asked Danny.

'Just tell her your daddy had a bit of a fall or something, and I'm popping over to pick her up.'

Jimmy gave Danny a few coins for the phone.

'You don't have to collect my granny, Jimmy, she's going to ring my Uncle Larry and get him to bring her over,' reported Danny when he got back.

'Your Uncle Larry?' said Jimmy. 'I thought your Dad and your Uncle Larry didn't get on well.'

Danny just shrugged his shoulders.

*   *   *

At last, a doctor arrived. She brought Danny and Jimmy into a private room; they were both as white as ghosts.

The doctor didn't tip-toe around them, 'Your father's had a stroke, Danny,' she said.

Danny looked at Jimmy.

'Do you know what that means, Danny?' she asked.

Danny's eyes were filling up. He nodded his head.

'He's just had a lot of tests,' she continued, 'but it's a little early to know exactly how well he will be when he wakes up.'

'What does she mean, Jimmy?'

Jimmy tried to answer, but he couldn't manage to get any words out.

The doctor told Danny and Jimmy that they could stay in the room, and it wasn't long before Granny and Uncle Larry popped their heads in the door.

Larry was in and out of the room like a yo-yo, trying to get more information for Danny and Granny, but the doctors just kept telling him that it was too soon for answers.

Although Mick was in intensive care, Danny and Granny were allowed to see him for a few minutes.

Danny was heartbroken when he saw his dad. Mick didn't look like the strong, bubbly figure that Danny was so used to. He looked fragile lying so still on his bed. Danny's tears began to flow, and he felt his granny's old and shaking hand grasp his, and that felt strange, but comforting.

Danny and Granny travelled home in the Bentley that night to Granny's flat, and although Danny was tired, he lay back on the new leather recliner and twiddled with the buttons all night, thinking about his dad, all alone in hospital.

Chapter 8

At the Hospital

Danny skipped school the next day and got the bus with his granny to the hospital.

Danny was in pretty good form going in. *Ah, sure, Dad will be sitting up reading the sports section of the morning papers,* he thought. But when they got to Mick's room, Danny was horrified to find that there was absolutely no change, and Mick was still unconscious.

They sat watching over Mick for ages and ages waiting for some sort of movement or something from him.

'Danny, pet!' said Granny. 'I'm gasping. Here's a few quid. Go and get me a cup of tea from the machine, and get yourself a drink, too.'

*   *   *

Danny kicked the drinks dispenser as if he was taking a forty-five on the Little Croker. It had swallowed one of his coins.

The machine wasn't co-operating and Danny cracked. He sat down on a chair beside it and cried with his face in his hands.

'Are you okay?' A girl, a little older than Danny, sat down on the chair beside him. She was quite a pretty girl, all dressed in Abercrombie.

Under normal circumstances, if a girl like this took any interest in Danny – and it hadn't ever happened yet – he would be *mortified* to be caught crying.

But right now Danny didn't really care what state he was in.

'I'm Trinity,' the girl said, 'What's your name?'

Danny removed his hands from his face and like a true young gentleman, snorted to clear his gunky nose.

'Danny. Danny Wilde.'

'Are you okay, Danny?' repeated Trinity. It seemed to Danny that this girl was a little too concerned, considering she didn't even know him.

'What do you think?' answered Danny cheekily.

Trinity turned her nose up at Danny, and in a very mature voice replied,

'Well, if you're going to be *rude!*'

Danny didn't like being called rude, and it didn't take him long to apologise to Trinity who had got up to leave.

'I'm sorry,' said Danny and he looked as if he meant it too.

Trinity sat back down, and Danny began to spill all his problems.

'My mam died when I was young,' he cried. 'I don't want to lose my dad too.'

Trinity put her arm around Danny.

'I know how you feel, Danny,' she

comforted. 'My father died a few years ago and my mother means the world to me.'

Danny stopped sobbing, partly because he felt a little guilty now that Trinity was probably starting to feel a little sad too, and partly (and more importantly) because he didn't want to look like too much of a softy.

'Who's your father's consultant?' Trinity queried.

'Eh!' Danny had to think, and while he was thinking, he also thought that was a really weird question for her to ask him. *How old is this girl, twenty-something?* he thought.

'Mrs Dawson, or something like that,' Danny remembered.

Just as Danny spoke her name, Dr Dawson appeared through a door at the far end of the corridor.

'That's her there!' said Danny.

'Don't worry about your father, Danny,' said Trinity.

'Why?' asked Danny.

Trinity stood up and walked towards Dr Dawson. She turned to Danny and smiled at him.

'She's my mother, and she's *really* good at her job!'

Then Trinity Dawson disappeared through the door at the end of the corridor, with her mother.

Danny sat on his chair for a few minutes thinking about Trinity.

He'd never really thought about a girl or girls, before. He only ever had time in his thoughts for football. Girls were a total waste of time!

But it seemed at that moment that Trinity Dawson had appeared to Danny for a special reason, and Danny was thankful for that – Trinity's words of comfort had made him feel better and hopeful. Maybe girls weren't that bad after all?

*   *   *

When Danny got back to his dad's room, his granny was standing outside the door.

'What kept you, Danny?' asked Granny

'I was just talking to the doctor's daughter!' replied Danny.

Normally an answer like that would trigger Granny's curiosity, but not this time. She had something important to tell Danny.

'Your daddy's awake!' she announced with a little smile.

'Savage!' said Danny, and he immediately thought of Trinity and her kind words.

'Can I go in and see him?'

'Not yet, pet,' said Granny. 'The doctors are in with him. Where's my tea?'

'Sorry, Granny. The machine was broken,' answered Danny with a huge smile. He was chuffed. *Dad's back!* he thought.

It wasn't long before the doctors came out and told Danny and his granny that they could go in and see Mick, but they warned them that he was very weak and had a long road to recovery.

Danny ran in ahead of his granny.

'Dad!' said Danny and he threw his arms around his father. There was no need for him to say any more as the hug said everything about how Danny was feeling, and that was the best medicine Mick could ask for.

When Danny sat back up onto the side of his dad's bed, he noticed that the right side of Mick's face was slightly droopier than the left and when Mick spoke, he struggled to get the words out properly.

Danny's reaction was one to be proud of. He knew a little about strokes as Splinter's grand-dad had suffered from a stroke the previous year.

'It's okay, Dad' said Danny. 'Just rest, sure we can talk later when you're feeling better.'

Danny and Granny went home in Jimmy's car that evening as Jimmy had popped up after work.

'What about your trial, Danny?' asked

Jimmy as they pulled up outside Shady Cedars.

Danny had completely forgotten about his trial.

'Did you ring them?' asked Jimmy.

'I forgot,' replied Danny. 'Anyway, my dad has the number somewhere. I don't know where he put it.'

'Ah, sure your daddy's on the mend now,' said Jimmy. 'That's more important.'

Just as Danny was getting out of the car, Jimmy remembered something.

'Oh! You needn't worry about tomorrow's game, Danny.'

Danny had been so occupied with his dad, that he had completely forgotten about Saturday's match.

'I forgot about that,' said Danny.

'Don't worry,' reiterated Jimmy. 'I phoned their manager today and told him everything. We're all in shock Danny. I thought it would be best if we got the game called off.'

'Good decision, Jimmy,' agreed Danny. 'So

we're playing them at the end of the season?'

Jimmy frowned. Danny knew instantly that Jimmy had made a hash of something.

'What's up, Jimmy?'

'They couldn't play the game then Danny, so we agreed to share the points.'

Danny closed the door, and rolled down his window to talk to his granny.

'I'll be in in a minute, Granny.'

'Are you *mad*, Jimmy?' asked Danny. 'Malachi's are at the bottom of the league. We'd have *slaughtered* them.'

Jimmy was sweating. He just wasn't up for all these management decisions, now that Mick was off the scene. *I shouldn't have turned down Paddy Flynn, the Under-15s coach, when he rang this morning and offered to help me out!* he thought.

After a moment Danny just said, 'Don't worry about it, Jimmy. We can still win the league.'

'Thanks, Danny. Of course we can, and sure your daddy getting better is more important than points.'

'But Jimmy!' shouted Danny, as Jimmy was driving off. '*You* can tell my dad, because I'm certainly not!'

Danny slept better that night on Granny's recliner and although he knew that there were hard times ahead, Jimmy was right, his dad was on the mend and things like football trials and league points did come second to family.

Chapter 9

Aylesbridge Close

Danny's dad improved a little over the weekend and when Danny went to the hospital after school on Monday he was surprised to see his dad and his Uncle Larry talking.

'All right, Uncle Larry?' greeted Danny as he sat on the side of his dad's bed.

'Daniel,' replied Larry.

'I was thinking about your trial this morning,' said Mick. He spoke slowly, but managed to make himself understood.

Danny wiped his dad's mouth with a handkerchief.

'No worries, Dad,' said Danny. 'There'll be other chances.'

'That's very mature of you, Daniel,' said Larry.

Then Larry went on to tell Danny what the two brothers had been talking about. The plan was for Danny to stay at Larry's house until his dad was well enough to look after him. Larry wouldn't oblige his brother under normal circumstances, but these were not normal times and Larry knew that it must have taken a lot for Mick to ask.

'Do I have to, Dad?' pleaded Danny.

'It's for the best, Danny,' said Larry. 'Your father needs plenty of proper hospital care and it's going to be quite a while yet before he's able to look after you again, or even come home.'

Danny didn't continue the dispute. One look at his dad and he realised that Larry's words were true, and his dad getting better – *Proper better*, thought Danny – was the main deal here.

It was agreed, against Danny's initial wishes, that Larry would collect Danny from his house the following Saturday as there was no game on that weekend. Until then he'd stay with his granny at Shady Cedars.

*   *   *

Saturday arrived and Uncle Larry and Jonathon arrived with it. They weren't in the Bentley this time, but in Regina's BMW x5. According to Regina that morning, you never know how a twelve-year-old boy will pack, or what junk he will want to drag along with him, so Larry brought the car with the bigger boot!

This was to the great disappointment of Splinter who was waiting anxiously on his wall to catch a glimpse of Larry's car, as never had a Bentley driven down his road before.

As Larry drove through Littlestown Lawns and by Danny's football pitch, Jonathon got a reality check as he looked out at broken trees and burnt patches of turf where night fires had been lit to warm the hands that held the cider cans that were still smouldering in the ashes.

'Take a good look, Jonathon,' said Larry with

a smirk on his face. 'This is how life could be for you, if you don't keep up your studies, or if you waste your time on pointless sports, or whatever these people get up to.'

Jonathon was embarrassed by his father's words.

'But this is where *you're* from, Dad, and *you're* successful,' he muttered bravely.

His dad gave no reply.

Larry had been warned by Regina not to leave the x5 unattended, so he sat reading his paper while Jonathon helped Danny bring his stuff out.

'You've a lot of posters on your walls,' observed Jonathon in Danny's room.

Danny's room was plastered from wall to wall with GAA posters, all of the Dubs, of course, and he'd have covered the ceiling as well if Mick had let him.

'Give us a hand, J?' asked Danny as he started to strip some of the posters to bring with him.

'"J"?' replied his cousin. 'Who's "J"?'

'You, ya' spanner!' laughed Danny. 'Jonathon takes ages to get out. Just "J" sounds cool!'

'Well! I suppose "J" is better than being called after a tool,' replied Jonathon and the two cousins laughed while rolling up Danny's favourite posters.

Finally, after Larry had read his paper twice from cover to cover, Danny Wilde locked the door of his home behind him.

'Come on, Heffo!' yelled Danny and his Jack Russell appeared out from under the hedge of next door's garden.

Danny opened his door and Heffo jumped straight up onto Regina's cream leather back seat.

'Get that mutt off the seat,' grunted Larry. 'You didn't say anything about a dog.'

'You didn't ask,' replied Danny and he closed his door. 'Down, Heffo. I'll keep him at my feet, he'll be no trouble.'

Jonathon was trying his very best not to laugh or even smile as he appreciated that his father was struggling with his cousin. Jonathon was beginning to think that Danny coming to stay at his house was going to be very exciting indeed!

With great discomfort, every now and then Larry looked into his rear view mirror to see a sight he was neither familiar with nor happy with – his son and Mick's son horseplaying together and having fun.

'That's enough, boys!' corrected Larry.

'We're only messing!' tutted Danny, and he caught a glimpse of Larry glaring at him in the mirror.

Jonathon never spoke a word to Danny for the rest of the journey and this made Danny very uncomfortable and very angry with his uncle. *My dad wouldn't treat me like that*, thought Danny. *Uncle Larry's nothing but a bully, and Jonathon is terrified of him.*

Danny pressed his nose against the glass and huffed steam all over it and then wiped it making squeaky noises that he knew would drive Larry mad.

Larry retaliated by putting on one of Regina's opera cds.

Heffo began to howl.

'Is that meant to be music? Your woman sounds in pain!' Danny giggled to Jonathon and he gave him a friendly elbow to try and make him join in.

Jonathon held back the smiles that were bursting at the seams of his mouth to get out.

Danny continued the banter as Uncle Larry was now humming along with the cd.

'Are there any puke bags in the back of this yoke, or what?'

That was too much for Jonathon – he burst out laughing and Danny joined in, raising the back seat noise above Larry's music.

Suddenly Larry turned off the music.

'We're here!' he announced, turning a corner into a cul-de-sac, and he opened Danny's window so as to give Danny a good, clear view of his new surroundings.

'Better view than the one earlier, Jonathon!' bragged Larry.

Danny had been enjoying looking out at the tall, bushy oak trees that lined the paths and the huge detached mansions behind their black pointed railings until Larry made that smart comment.

Danny pressed the button and his window came up. Jonathon noticed his reaction. His father had hurt his cousin, who he was just beginning to really like, and that made Jonathon properly ashamed of his father.

'Your new home, Danny, well – temporary new home!' said Larry as two very tall and very wide black iron gates automatically opened and the x5 slowly crunched along the gravel driveway of number ten Aylesbridge Close, up to a house that looked to Danny as big as a hotel.

'Wow!' gasped Danny and he looked at Jonathon and smiled.

Regina came down the granite steps with Earl, her shitzu, in her arms.

As soon as Danny opened the door, Heffo jumped out and ran across the driveway and leapt up onto Regina's dress barking his brains out at Earl.

Earl snarled down at Heffo, as if to say, *Shut it, mongrel, this is my home!*

Danny grabbed Heffo and apologised to his aunt who was shaking like a leaf.

'Jonathon, bring Daniel around the side to the garage, and make up a bed for his dog!' instructed Larry.

'Yes, Dad!' said Jonathon promptly. He knew that Danny was off to a bad start already.

'What about my stuff, Uncle Larry?' asked Danny while trying to muzzle Heffo under his armpit.

Larry gave Danny one of the looks that he was getting very familiar with, very quickly.

'I'll get it later, I suppose,' he said, and set off after his cousin.

Jonathon and Danny made a cosy bed for Heffo out of a cardboard box and an old picnic blanket that was just lying around in the garage.

'You lay down there, Heffo,' said Danny. 'I'll bring you for a walk later.' Then he looked at Jonathon and laughed. 'We probably won't even have to leave this place for a walk, it's that big.'

Danny stared all around at the gardens as Jonathon led him to the back door of the house.

He had never seen a place like this before. It was like something his granny would watch on one of her boring 'great houses and their gardens' programmes.

There were at least three lawns, not just one, and long, high, old, stone walls covered in thick, fleshy ivy surrounded the gardens.

There were granite steps leading up to the first lawn and a winding cobbled pathway curved around the dense, shrubby borders and then cut across the centre of the lawn to a big, mossy, cobbled circle with a large bronze statue of a boy and a girl holding an umbrella; crystal clear water was trickling down their umbrella and gently splashing into the pool that surrounded them.

'Wow!' gasped Danny to Jonathon. Danny had never given two hoots about gardens or fountains or, well, things that only grown-ups thought about, but then he had never seen such a beautiful place as this, and to imagine that people actually lived here, was unimaginable to Danny.

'Would you like to see the tennis court?' asked Jonathon. He didn't mean to brag like his father would, he was just trying to be a good, polite host to his cousin.

'No *way!*' said Danny. 'You have a *tennis court?*'

Jonathon led Danny down the cobbled path, across the lawn by the fountain, down more steps into another smaller garden with a circular lawn, and through a big archway covered in twining, thorny rose bushes and there, at the very end of the last garden, was a tennis court.

Animal! thought Danny. *This place is like being on holidays!*

Chapter 10

Danny's New Room

Uncle Larry had roped Lowry into helping
him drag all Danny's stuff up to his room.
Number ten Aylesbridge Close had seven bed-
rooms, so finding a spare room for Danny
wasn't a problem, but the colours that Aunt
Regina had it painted during the week would
turn out to be a *big* problem for Danny.

Jonathon was now giving Danny the tour of
the house, as he knew that the longer he kept
Danny out of his mother's way after the driveway incident the more time she would have to
cool down and the less chance there was of
Heffo being put into boarding kennels.

Regina appeared from one of the many
upstairs corridors, with Earl in pursuit.

'Oh! There you are, boys. Jonathon, darling, show Danny to his room. All his things are there.'

It was lucky that Regina wasn't present when Danny opened the door to his new bedroom.

Danny just stood at the door and his face and his unusual silence said everything about how he felt about Regina's choice of colours.

'What's up, Danny?' asked Jonathon. 'Mum had it painted when she heard you were coming to stay. Do you not like it?'

Jonathon didn't understand the impression the room with its bright white walls and ceiling, gleaming red window ledges and new red curtains was making on Danny.

'Cork!' said Danny.

Now Jonathon thought that the lingering paint fumes were eating Danny's brain – what did he mean 'Cork'?

'I can't sleep in a room decked out in Cork colours! You have to help me to cover these walls, J. Thank God I brought some posters!'

'You're mad!' laughed Jonathon.

'I will be if I have to sleep in here. This will be like being all on my own in the middle of Cork supporters with all the red and white around me!'

Danny and Jonathon unrolled the posters and covered the walls. When Jonathon saw the relief and pure contentment on Danny's face as the last blue poster went over his bed, he thought how wonderful it was to have Danny in his home and how he, too, would like to be as passionate about something as Danny was about his football.

Chapter 11

The Kickabout

Later that day, Danny persuaded Jonathon to have a kickabout, as Larry and Regina had gone into town.

Danny was well impressed with Jonathon. Okay, he hadn't the foggiest notion about the rules or even how to play the game, but Danny could see that his cousin had natural ability; he probably inherited his dormant talent from Larry.

'There's fifteen players on a team,' explained Danny.

Jonathon nodded his head.

'Right! Fifteen, like rugby. They play rugby at our school. Father's always on at me to join the team, but it looks a bit rough to me.'

Danny just stared at Jonathon, and when his cousin was finished babbling on about rugby, Danny let loose.

'Rugby!' he screeched. 'Gaelic football is *nothing* like rugby. Rugby is played by a bunch of big, hairy wrestlers who just want to chase each other up and down the pitch. No way!' insisted Danny. 'No comparison *at all*. GAA is all about skill and pace. None of that cuddling each other in circles stuff in GAA!'

Jonathon kept his mouth shut for the rest of Danny's tutorial session.

Danny had sold the whole package of GAA to Jonathon, and the fact that he expressed how good Jonathon could actually be at this magnificent sport just got Jonathon fired up inside.

'Can I join your team, Danny?' asked Jonathon. He was nearly shaking with excitement. Danny was gobsmacked.

'What about your dad?'

The moment of madness had passed for

Jonathon – of course he couldn't join Danny's team. Larry would rather have his eyes poked out by magpies than let his son play for Littlestown Crokes.

Danny knew that he was partly to blame for raising Jonathon's hopes and then dashing them again by mentioning the dreaded name.

'You could join the team without your dad knowing,' he suggested cheekily.

Jonathon just laughed. But it was a dismissive laugh, not a happy one.

'Seriously! You could!' persisted Danny.

'Father would kill me if he found out, and how would I be able to play without him wondering what I was up to?'

'Invent something,' said Danny.

Jonathon just shook his head.

'Go on, J.' Danny wasn't going to give up on this. 'Look! You want to play for my team. We need a good player, because my dad kicked a player off the team last week, and you're a savage player. It's meant to be.'

After a few minutes of total silence, Jonathon just looked up at Danny. Danny had chosen his words of encouragement well.

'I could tell Father that I've joined the debate club at school or maybe the drama club.'

Danny jumped up and kicked the ball high into the sky.

'That's it so. You'll be going to your club on Tuesdays and Thursdays and Saturday afternoons, and we'd better come up with something for Halloween too!'

'Halloween?' repeated Jonathon.

Danny told Jonathon all about Halloween and how his dad and Jimmy had organised a trip down to Wexford for the team.

'My dad has a friend down in Kimuldridge who manages the local under-14s team.'

Jonathon was all ears. The rewards of joining Danny's team were getting better by the minute.

'But won't your dad still be in hospital?'

'Yeah! But he told Jimmy not to cancel the

trip, so it's still on. We're going to stay overnight in the local hotel. It's going to be savage. There's a youth disco on that night.'

'Savage!' said Jonathon. Now he was beginning to talk like Danny.

'Yeah!' said Danny. 'But that's not the half of it. The next morning we're playing the under-14s in a friendly.'

'But they're older than us, is that fair?' asked Jonathon. Now Danny's competitiveness was rubbing off on him!

'Yeah! But that's okay. It's only a friendly and my dad said that because there's a break of a few weeks before the last game against Barnfield, the experience of it all will pay off.'

Danny stood back up to get his ball.

'We'll go into the hospital tomorrow and tell my dad that you're joining the team,' said Danny.

'Won't he mind?' asked Jonathon.

'Don't worry. He'll be delighted that you're joining the team, especially behind your dad's back.'

The two boys shook hands and then continued their game of football.

It was a hectic day for Danny and he was wrecked going to bed that night. Even though he was surrounded by the red and white colours of the Cork team, his posters did the trick and he slept well in his first night in number ten Aylesbridge Close.

Chapter 12

Can 'J' Join the Team?

The next morning, Danny was last to wake and as he pulled his curtains open, the first thing he caught sight of was Uncle Larry and Aunt Regina on the tennis court.

Animal! thought Danny. He would never have thought that Aunt Regina would be into sport, but there she was in her white, frilly Slazenger mini-dress and her sun visor, running poor Larry around the court.

Danny sat on the big bay windowsill for ages watching the very one-sided match and it didn't take him long to figure out that there was no way that it was Uncle Larry's idea to fork out for the tennis court.

Larry must have noticed Danny in the

window because right in the middle of a game he just threw in the towel, and unfortunately for Danny, that was the end of his entertainment for the morning.

Danny legged it downstairs and out to the kitchen. He desperately wanted to congratulate Aunt Regina in front of Larry as they came in from the garden.

Jonathon and Lowry were already finished their breakfast when Danny rushed into the kitchen.

Larry was first in the back door. He was so drenched with sweat that he looked like he'd just run the marathon, and his face was like a beetroot.

Danny kept quiet, while Larry downed a whole litre of tropical juice.

In waltzed Aunt Regina. *Total respect!* thought Danny. *Not a bother on her. She looks like she could actually run the marathon.*

'Good morning, kids,' smiled Regina. 'Sleep well, Daniel?'

'Like a log!' answered Danny. 'Good game out there. You should play for a tennis club,' suggested Danny.

Aunt Regina was delighted, but Larry let out a big belch. That was what he thought of Danny's remark.

That evening, after dinner, Aunt Regina dropped Danny and Jonathon into the hospital.

Mick was thrilled to see that Danny and Jonathon were getting on so well.

'How's your mam and dad?' Mick asked Jonathon politely. His speech was quickly improving.

'They're fine, Uncle Mick,' answered Jonathon.

It wasn't long before GAA took over the conversation as Mick didn't really know what to say to his nephew, considering he didn't actually know anything about him.

'Everything all right at the club, Danny? Is Jimmy managing okay?' asked Mick anxiously.

Danny wondered if Jimmy had told his dad

about the Malachi's game blunder, so he didn't really answer his question, but his face must have given him away.

Mick chuckled.

'Is it really that bad, son? Don't worry, Jimmy told me about his mistake last week. Just keep an eye on him, Danny. We all know that Jimmy's not the best with management, but with your help we can still win the league.'

Those words perked Danny up, and he felt it was a good time to discuss Jonathon's desire to join the team.

'Eh, Dad? Jonathon's a really good player, and he wants to join the team.'

If Jonathon wasn't present at that very moment, Mick Wilde would probably have fallen out of the bed laughing. But one look at his nephew's face when Danny spoke and he knew how desperately Jonathon awaited a positive response.

'Really?' said Mick.

'Yeah! We've being playing out in his back

garden and he's good and he's dying to join us.'

Mick knew that he had to be *very* cautious with his nephew's desire to join the team, but he also knew that eventually, the Larry factor had to be brought into the conversation.

'And what does your daddy think of all this?' asked Mick.

Jonathon looked at Danny, and Danny looked at Jonathon.

That was enough for Mick.

'How are you going to join the team if your dad doesn't even know that you like football?'

'His dad won't let him,' interrupted Danny.

'Did you even ask him?' quizzed Mick.

Jonathon just shook his head, and then mumbled, 'No point.'

Danny had got it all wrong. He thought that his dad would be up for getting one over on Larry. But what Danny didn't realise was that when it came to Larry's kids, Mick Wilde had absolutely no interest in playing games. Family business is serious business, and Danny and

Jonathon left the hospital gutted as Mick explained that the only way Jonathon could join the team was with Larry's consent.

Chapter 13

The Plan

Poor Jonathon was as quiet as a mouse going home on the bus.

Danny tried to start a few conversations, but only got one-word answers from his cousin.

Unlike Jonathon, who was just gutted, Danny was gutted *and* annoyed. He had *really* thought that his dad would go along with their plan behind Larry's back.

'We can still do it,' said Danny.

For the first time since they'd boarded the bus, Jonathon turned his head and looked at Danny.

'How?'

'Well, you were willing to go behind your dad's back so I don't see why I shouldn't do the same.'

My dad never told me the whole truth about his troubles with Larry, thought Danny, and that was his justification.

Now Jonathon was all ears.

'Go on.'

Danny explained the plan to Jonathon. Just like Larry, Mick wasn't going to know anything. Danny would get Splinter in on the act. Splinter would tell Jimmy that he knew a boy from his swimming club who wanted to join the team and all Jonathon had to do was turn up on Tuesday for training, providing he fooled Larry.

'But your dad will know everything when he comes back to the club!' worried Jonathon.

'I know that,' said Danny. 'But if we just concentrate on now and win the league and you've helped us, we might be able to get my dad to reconsider.'

Jonathon liked that. It definitely made sense, and even if all failed, at least he would have had a chance to try it out.

By Tuesday, all was going smoothly to plan. Jonathon had put on a great display of drama about the new club at his school and Larry had fallen for it, hook, line and sinker as he thought it would mean his son would have less time to spend with Danny.

Splinter was buzzing with the thoughts of being allowed in on the action, and – being a James Bond fanatic – he felt like he was on a secret mission himself.

Splinter got the ball rolling on his end too and when Jimmy asked his friend's name. Splinter simply replied, 'J.'

Danny supplied Jonathon with some training gear and an old pair of football boots that he had collected from home on his lunch break.

It wasn't just clothes he provided, but also a lesson in how to look and act the part so as not to draw any suspicion.

The two cousins separated before they reached the Little Croker, but before they did, Danny had a few words of advice for his cousin.

'You wait here for a few minutes, J, and then make your way over to us.'

'Right, Danny,' nodded Jonathon.

Jonathon was dead nervous, and he was beginning to question his sanity – he would never have *dreamt* of doing anything as crazy as this before he hooked up with Danny.

Danny strolled over to the training area. Jimmy had everything set up nicely, and most of the team had turned up for training.

Splinter put his secret agent role into action and greeted Danny.

'What's the story, Danny? I've a new player for the team. He's coming up tonight. Is that okay?'

'Animal,' replied Danny. 'Is he any good?'

'Savage,' smiled Splinter. 'Here he is now.'

Everybody, especially Jimmy, watched eagerly as Jonathon shuffled his way across the playing field with his training bag slung over his left shoulder.

Danny had told him to look a bit more

relaxed and sort of cool when he was walking, but he didn't anticipate that Jonathon's version of relaxed and cool would make him look like a cowboy walking across the pitch.

'The state of him!' laughed Paddy Timmons.

'What's the story, Spittser?' greeted Jonathon.

Now everyone was laughing at Splinter because they thought 'J' was slagging him.

Danny had a little word in Jonathon's ear and advised his cousin not to bother with the fitting-in plan.

Jonathon may have made a poor first impression on the team, but he certainly made a lasting impression on Jimmy during training. Jonathon was a natural at GAA and he proved that by playing a stormer in training.

Jimmy was dead keen to get him signed and the sooner the better as it takes a week for registration to go through and there were only a few games left in the league.

Jimmy got the ball rolling.

'So, Jason, is it?' asked Jimmy.

'Just J, Da,' answered Splinter on Jonathon's behalf.

'Sorry, J. So, what do you think? Interested in signing for us?'

'Absolutely!' answered Jonathon.

'Super. Good man. Mick will be delighted. I'll just have to get a form for you to sign and then you'll be okay to play in a week or two.'

Danny had been hovering around behind Jimmy; as soon as he heard his dad's name and forms mentioned in the one sentence, he jumped straight into the conversation.

'Eh! Jimmy. I'll get a form from the house for him.'

'Nice one, Danny!' said Jimmy. 'If you get it back to me, J, as quick as you can, I'll send it off.'

'Why don't we get the form now, Jimmy, and you can fill out your bit and then put it in an addressed envelope for J, and he can send it straight away, because I'm not going to be back at my house until Thursday.'

Jimmy, being Jimmy, thought that was a super idea and did exactly what Danny had suggested, and so that was the paperwork taken care of.

Chapter 14

The Match Against Castle Village

Jonathon continued to impress everyone at training on Thursday, as Danny seized every opportunity to coach him when Uncle Larry and Aunt Regina weren't around. He wasn't going to be playing in Saturday's match away against Castle Village, though, as his registration hadn't gone through yet.

Jonathon sat and watched as all the other players togged out for the game before Danny gave Jimmy the nod for the pre-match talk.

'Right lads! Listen in,' announced Jimmy, trying his best to sound like Mick. 'OK, boys! Em, well, as you all know, it's the first game since Danny's dad took ill, and I know you're all missing your manager, but I'm sure he's sitting up in his bed now, willing us to win.'

Not bad, thought Danny, *but it needs a bit more bite to get them going.*

'Nice one, Jimmy,' said Danny. 'We have to go out there, lads, and give it everything for my dad! Jimmy's right, he probably is sitting in his bed, willing us to win, but we don't stand a chance if we don't will *ourselves* to win!'

The team let out a big roar!

He's good, thought Jimmy, nodding his head. *Yeah! A real chip off the old block.*

'Then let's get out there and bring the points home!' yelled Danny, and on that note, Mick Wilde's team marched out of the away dressing rooms and into battle for their absent general.

Under Danny's watchful eye, Jimmy had selected the same team layout that had beaten St Agnes' boys. The only change he made was to bring in Anto Farrell to replace Sean Dempsey, the player that Mick had kicked off the team.

Anto would have preferred to slot back into his left corner full back position that Kevin Kinsella now had, but Jimmy thought that if Mick was present he would probably have left Kevin there as he had played really well in the last game.

Littlestown Crokes must have been inspired by Danny's words as straight from the throw-in they absolutely bombarded the home team's defence, knocking over point after point. After twenty minutes, Danny's team was winning by five points to nil, of which Danny had scored two points.

Jimmy was thrilled with himself. Here he was, all on his own, holding the fort while Mick was away, and everything was running smoothly.

Jonathon thought that Jimmy was dead funny, running up the line and cheering his boys on when the Crokes burst forward and then running back down the line, chewing his fingers, when Castle Village got the ball back down the pitch!

The referee blew his whistle for half time and the Crokes were still winning, but only by three points now as towards the end of the first half, Castle Village had made a bit of a comeback; the score was seven points to four points in the Crokes' favour.

As all the players eagerly ate their oranges, Danny noticed that Jimmy was very quiet.

'Any half-time words, Jimmy?' he whispered.

Jimmy took a big breath. It was obvious now to everyone that poor Jimmy had a dose of the jitters and his nerves were beginning to let him down.

'Right lads!' trembled Jimmy. That didn't do the trick as only a few players even heard him speak.

'Will yiz *shut up*!' roared Danny with more than a hint of Mick Wilde's tone in his voice.

Now everyone tuned in.

'Thanks, Danny,' smiled Jimmy. 'Just keep going at them, lads. You started great, you let them come back at you a bit easy towards the end of that half.'

'It's Anto!' shouted Alan Whelan, the centre half back. 'He's losing everything in midfield and Danny's having to cover for him all the time!'

'Shut up, Wheelo!' retaliated Anto.

'Will yiz give it up!' shouted Splinter. Splinter felt sorry for his dad. He was mortified as he knew Jimmy would have just stood there and let the two boys rip into each other if he hadn't spoken up.

For the first time ever, Splinter realised just how important Mick Wilde really was to the team, and also to his dad. Jimmy just wasn't cut out for management without Mick.

As the referee blew his whistle, it was up to Danny to get the team's spirits up again, but he knew that even if they managed to scrape a win out of this game, the hard fact was that the dismissal of Sean Dempsey had fractured the strength of the team and that fracture had to be repaired or the last match against Barnfield wouldn't even count.

The solution to the problem was simple in Danny's mind. Jonathon – J – was the man for the job!

*   *   *

On the sidelines Jonathon was mesmerised by his cousin's talent. *Danny's just dynamite*, thought Jonathon as he watched him play the second half out of his skin.

Danny Wilde wasn't just playing out of his skin, he was playing out of his age too. He just controlled the whole second half of the game – he looked like an under-16s player among a younger and less experienced group of players.

'Raw talent!' Jimmy kept turning to Jonathon and saying.

Jonathon was itching to jump up and announce to everyone that Danny was his cousin and he was proud of that. But he couldn't or that would be the end for him before he even had his chance to try to be as good as his cousin.

Following Danny's lead, his team-mates lifted their game. Although they only scored two more points in the second half, crucially to their title hopes they battled and scrapped to prevent the home team from scoring at all, and the game ended nine points to four points in favour of the Crokes.

Chapter 15

A Close Shave

That night, Danny and Jonathon went into the hospital to see Mick, and fill him in on the match that day.

Danny did all the filling in as Jonathon wasn't even supposed to have been there; Jonathon just sat on the edge of Mick's bed pretending to be as gobsmacked as his uncle as Danny re-enacted the whole game for his dad.

Mick was thrilled to bits.

'Only two games to go, son!' said Mick and he clenched his right fist in the air.

At that moment Danny was the happiest he had been since Mick was taken ill.

There was his dad, smiling and punching the air. A simple task, but one that Mick couldn't have managed straight after his stroke.

The nurse with the medicine trolley came into Mick's room and so Danny and Jonathon did a disappearing act to the vending machine to get some drinks.

On their way back to the room, the cousins chuckled about how Jonathon had to put on an act in front of Mick while Danny described the match.

'I nearly butted in a few times!' laughed Jonathon as they got to Mick's door.

'Shush!' hushed Danny and he stopped in his tracks and stooped down below the door and peeped in through the glass.

'I don't believe it!'

'What's wrong?' asked Jonathon, afraid that something was wrong with Mick.

'It's Jimmy!' said Danny. 'Come on back around the corner.'

Jonathon hid well out of sight while Danny went back in to his dad's room.

'All right, Jimmy!' said Danny, acting cool.

'Howya, Danny!' replied Jimmy. 'I just popped in to tell your daddy about the stormer you played today, but it seems that you beat me to it.'

'Where's Jonathon?' interrupted Mick.

'Emmmm ... Uncle Larry's picking us up and he's, eh, he's ... he's after ringing him on his phone to say he's down in the car park already, so he's just gone down to tell him to hang on for me.'

'You better not keep him waiting, son. There's a good lad,' yawned Mick. The medicine was starting to take effect.

Danny thought that all was left was a simple goodbye to his dad, and that would be that, but Jimmy said, 'Did you tell your daddy about the new player, Danny?'

'New player?' asked Mick.

Danny had to be as quick as a flash with his answer.

'Oh! Splinter's mate?'

'Who's this?' quizzed Mick.

Luckily for Danny, Jimmy was dying to tell Mick something that Danny hadn't already beaten him to, so he went on and on about his son's friend from swimming who was interested in joining because a player had left. Jimmy even called him 'Jason'.

'I better get off, Dad,' interrupted Danny.

'All the best, son,' said Mick.

'See you on Tuesday night, Danny,' said Jimmy.

Danny disappeared out the door and when he told Jonathon just how close a shave it was, the two boys agreed that Jonathon shouldn't go to the hospital with Danny again.

Chapter 16

'*Operation Larry*'

The next game for the Crokes couldn't come quickly enough for Jonathon Wilde. The game was all he could think about when he was in school. He couldn't sleep at night and he couldn't even go to the bathroom without thinking about playing his first game for Danny's team. He was obsessed.

Even Danny noticed that all his cousin wanted to do was talk GAA, play GAA, and watch GAA. So that's exactly what they did.

When his parents were out, Jonathon practised and practised and at night he watched Danny's GAA dvds on his portable dvd player (under the covers, in case his dad came in and caught him).

But unfortunately for Jonathon, Jimmy announced at Thursday night's training that there would be no match on Saturday.

'A walk-over!' cheered Jimmy.

All the boys cheered in celebration. Normally they hated walk-overs, but at this stage in the league they were feeling the pressure and they knew that it was more precious points in the bag.

The team they were supposed to play, Willow View, was at the bottom of the league and had cancelled because a bunch of the players had lost interest and gone off to play soccer, and there was no point in turning up with half a team.

As expected by everybody, Barnfield won their second last game, and so Jonathon's hopes were pinned on the friendly in Wexford against Kimuldridge under-14s on 1 November – he really hoped he'd pull off a good enough performance to make it into the starting fifteen for the title game against Barnfield on the Little

Croker on 8 November.

The following week flew by and Jonathon still hadn't managed to pluck up enough courage to tackle the Larry problem and book himself a seat on the coach to Wexford.

On Saturday night, only six days before the trip, Larry and Regina were rushing around the house, trying to get themselves ready for a night at the opera. They were late because Larry had an emergency meeting with a client that day and it ran late.

Danny kept hassling Jonathon to come up with something, but no matter how much Jonathon racked his brain, the truth was, the thought of actually going on a trip away from home overnight without telling his parents petrified him.

He'd lied about joining a club at school and he'd gone to training and to matches instead, but this was different. This kind of lie was off the scale!

While Larry and Regina were arguing

upstairs, Jonathon, Lowry and Danny were crashed out in front of the telly in the living room.

The door bell rang, and Lowry jumped up.

'I'll get it.'

'We weren't moving,' laughed Jonathon, and he reached out to Danny for a high five.

Somehow, the cousins' high five turned into a wrestling match on the floor. Danny had his leg wrapped around Jonathon and had him in a head lock. He had taken off his socks and was trying to stick his smelly toes into Jonathon's nose when somebody very special from his recent past walked into the room.

'Danny!' said the person, and she laughed.

It was Trinity Dawson – she was a friend of Lowry's!

Danny turned pink and let Jonathon go.

'All right!' he said.

Lowry stood beside Trinity with her jaw hanging open.

'Do you two know each other? Like, *how* do

you two know each other? You *can't*. It's impossible. He's not from around here, and like, you haven't been around in *ages*, Trinity, so you can't know who he is!'

It was just too much for Lowry. The thought of one of her friends knowing that Danny was her cousin was killing her, but when Trinity and Danny explained how they had previously met, Lowry calmed down.

Just a bit of bad luck! thought Lowry. *It happens!*

Lowry dragged Trinity upstairs to her room.

If we're stuck in with those two clowns all night, there's no way I'm exposing my friend to Danny any more than I have to, thought Lowry.

Jonathon couldn't resist slagging Danny.

'She fancies you!' he laughed.

'Get lost,' muttered Danny.

'You're going red. You must fancy her too!'

Jonathon was now rolling around the floor in stitches.

'Shut up, ye muppet!'

Danny tried to look serious, but he just

couldn't resist a small smile.

Larry popped his head in the door.

'What's so funny?' he asked

Jonathon nearly leapt to his feet.

'Nothing, Dad!'

'Larry! I can't find the camera,' called Regina from upstairs.

'That woman!' muttered Larry as he hurried out the door.

Danny jumped back on Jonathon's case about the trip.

'You're going to *have* to come up with something or you won't be going.'

'We could ask Trinity to help us,' suggested Jonathon.

'How is Trinity going to help us? And why would she?'

Jonathon just smiled at Danny and nodded his head.

Danny went red again.

Jonathon was right. Trinity must have had a soft spot for Danny because when they asked for her help during one of her snack visits to the kitchen, she was all for helping them come up with a plan to get Jonathon on the trip.

Danny, Jonathon and Trinity spent most of the evening going over and over what they called, 'Operation Larry' while Lowry sat tutting.

'It won't work,' she said. 'You're all going to be crucified when Father finds out.'

When Larry and Regina finally got home, Trinity didn't waste any time in putting 'Operation Larry' into action.

Larry and Regina were in the kitchen having a nightcap.

Trinity walked in with Lowry, while Danny and Jonathon crept down to the bottom of the staircase to listen in.

'I'm off, guys,' said Trinity.

'See you, petal!' said Regina.

Larry just nodded.

Just as Trinity was heading out the door, she turned to Regina and said, 'Oh! Regina, when you see Jonathon could you tell him that my brother Sebastian is having a sleepover on Friday night, if he wants come over?'

Regina looked at Larry.

'That's Halloween night.'

Larry nodded.

'Bye!' said Trinity and she left the rest to Lady Luck.

Danny and Jonathon waited in desperate anticipation.

'Danny's away with his club that night, isn't he?' asked Regina.

Larry laughed.

'That's right! Just imagine the peace we'd have with those two out of the house.'

There was nothing said after that, but Danny and Jonathon looked at each other and smiled. They knew that 'Operation Larry' was going well, but it still needed a few final touches.

The following day, Regina mentioned the sleepover to Jonathon.

Jonathon played along, pretending that he didn't know anything about it.

'I didn't know that you and Trinity's brother were friends,' said Regina.

'We weren't until I joined this new club in school. He seems okay.'

Larry walked into the room just as Jonathon spoke.

'Would you like to stay over at his house on Halloween?' asked Regina.

Those were the critical words that Jonathon was waiting to hear.

Jonathon turned towards Larry.

'I suppose so. It might give me a chance to get to know some of his friends.'

Those words were music to Larry's ears. In Larry's mind, Jonathon and Danny had spent a lot of time together over the past few weeks, and Larry didn't like that at all. So the idea of Jonathon having a sleepover at Sebastian's house was very appealing!

Little did Larry and Regina know that they

had just given the green light to 'Operation Larry'!

Chapter 17

According to Plan

The two cousins had to be very careful not to slip up and say anything that might draw suspicion on the morning of their trip, and so they kept their distance from each other.

Everything was going nicely to plan. Larry said his goodbyes to Jonathon at breakfast, as he knew that he'd probably be gone by the time he'd get home from work. He left in fairly good form, probably because he didn't have Danny glaring across the table at him.

Danny was deliberately still in bed.

The coach wasn't leaving Littlestown until five o'clock, which suited Danny and Jonathon perfectly.

Danny said his goodbyes to Regina and

Jonathon at lunch time. He made out that his coach was leaving at two o'clock, and he wanted to go home first to check on his dad's house.

As Danny strolled out the driveway, little did his aunt realise that stuffed into his training bag were Jonathon's good clothes for the disco.

The only thing that Danny was telling the truth about was the fact that he was going home first. But not just to check on the house – Jonathon's training bag was in Danny's house, and that had to be collected.

At three o'clock Jonathon started banging on Lowry's bedroom door.

'Come on, Lowry!' he yelled. 'It's time.'

Lowry left him waiting there for a few minutes. She resented the fact that Trinity had roped her into being a part of 'Operation Larry' and wanted Jonathon to know that although she would help, it would be under protest.

The door opened.

Jonathon had his mobile phone ready.

'Mum's in the back garden. I'll ring you in about two minutes.'

Lowry just stuck her tongue out at Jonathon and waved her phone in front of him. Then she went out to the garden.

'It's freezing out here, Mum. Would you like me to fetch you a cup of tea?'

Regina was planting some primroses in the rockery.

'That would be lovely, darling.'

Lowry looked up to the bedroom window, where Jonathon was peeping out.

Immediately her phone rang.

'Hi, Trinity!' said Lowry, slightly above her normal tone, just for her mother's benefit.

'Okay! Yep! Super! I'll be over in a while. I've just got to make my poor freezing Mum a cup of tea. She's out in the garden fiddling with her rockery.'

Lowry wasn't surprised to notice that Regina was listening, and she turned up her performance. She'd always wanted to be an actress.

'I'm not bringing brat features with me. Mum can drop him over later.'

'What's that, darling?' interrupted Regina.

Lowry made a big huff.

'Hold on, Trinity – nothing Mum!'

'If you're going over to Trinity's now, you can bring your brother with you.'

'*Muuum!*' screeched Lowry.

Lowry said goodbye in a cross voice and hung up her phone. Jonathon smiled down at her from the bedroom window.

'Operation Larry' had moved to the next level.

* * *

Regina gave Jonathon his instructions going out the door and a big, sloppy, motherly kiss.

'Don't cause any trouble, darling,' insisted Regina. 'What time will you be home tomorrow? Let me know and I'll pick you up. Have you got your phone?'

'I'll be okay, Mum. I'll make my own way

home, I'm nearly thirteen,' huffed Jonathon.

'I'll ring you tonight, darling, to see if you're okay!' called Regina as Jonathon crunched across the driveway.

* * *

Danny was thrilled when he saw Jonathon getting off the bus in Littlestown.

'Animal!' cheered Danny and he threw his arm around his cousin.

'See!' he said. 'Piece of cake. Here's your bag, I've put your clothes in it.'

Jonathon just smiled. He was feeling a little bit sick with what he had just done, but there was no going back now.

The atmosphere was buzzing on the coach, as all the boys were excited about their trip. Jimmy sat up at the front with the driver and some parents who had come along to help supervise.

He spoke into a cordless microphone, 'Okay lads, settle down. Anyone caught messing will be kicked off the bus!' chuckled Jimmy. He was in his element.

'Sing us a song, Jimmy?' shouted Danny.

Jimmy went red.

'Ah! Go on, Jimmy!' Danny kept up the pressure.

'Jimmy! Jimmy! Jimmy!' Danny and all the boys started banging on the head rests of the seats and chanting Jimmy's name.

The coach driver looked at Jimmy as if to say, *You'd better do something to calm them down.*

Poor Jimmy hadn't got a hope in hell. Even with his microphone, he had no chance of raising his volume above the sound of eighteen chanting boys.

Eventually the chanting faded away and all the boys settled down, much to Jimmy's relief.

The coach was stopped at traffic lights in the centre of town, when Danny let out an unmerciful roar from down the back.

'There's Jason Sherlock!'

All the boys on the left side of the coach leapt

up off their seats and wrestled their way to the windows on the right side of the coach.

Jimmy – who might be expected to be trying to restore order by getting the boys back into their seats – was the first to stick his nose up against a window for a glimpse at the Dublin GAA star getting out of a car across the road.

The coach driver started to panic as eighteen boys, headed up by Danny, were now banging on the windows, chanting, 'Jayo! Jayo! Jayo!'

When Jason Sherlock waved across at the Littlestown Crokes' players and gave them a big thumbs-up, Danny whipped off his jacket to reveal his Dublin jersey and pinned himself against the window, in respect for one of his all-time heroes.

Chapter 18

A Night in Wexford

Two hours after departure, all the passen-
gers and the driver arrived safe and sound
at the hotel in Kimuldridge.

Jonathon's nerves had settled down and,
along with every other boy, he was looking forward to the night ahead, but not quite as much
as the match the following morning. It was
going to be his big debut!

Danny, Jonathon and Splinter were sharing a
room. The three pals joked and messed and
had pillow fights and water fights and danced
to the music on Splinter's I-PAL, getting themselves all hyped up and buzzing for the disco.
They were so excited that you'd think that they
had never been in a hotel room before!

It's true to say that Splinter and Danny didn't have much hotel room experience under their belts, but Jonathon Wilde had been in the best hotels all over the world, and yet no matter how much money his father had splashed out on them, Jonathon thought that this room was the best he'd ever stayed in.

When the partying was over it was time for the pals to get down to the serious business of showering, tooth brushing and – finally and most importantly – hair gelling.

It's said that girls spend more time than boys getting all done up for a night out, but Jimmy must have made at least three trips up to their room to tell them that the disco had started, and still, all three were combing and twiddling and spiking lashings of the magic green gel into their hair.

Finally Danny, Jonathon and Splinter marched through the doors of the hotel basement disco room. The three of them stopped and stared – they hadn't expected to see so many girls. There were plenty of local lads too, but four walls were lined with girls.

'Are we dancing?' asked Jonathon.

Splinter burst out laughing.

'Get a grip!' said Danny.

Jonathon couldn't understand the hostile reaction to his suggestion. After all, they *were* at a disco.

'We're not here to dance, ye muppet!' laughed Danny.

Splinter put his hand on Jonathon's shoulder.

'Look around the room and tell me what you see,' he said.

'Girls?'

'Correct!' said Splinter. 'Do you seriously think that I'm going to waste my time bopping around the dancefloor when I could be putting my chat-up lines into action? Follow me, boys!' instructed Splinter and he led the way with Danny and Jonathon in stitches behind him.

Splinter's chat-up lines didn't turn out to be as good as he thought; after the reaction he got from the girls, Danny and Jonathon didn't even bother trying to talk to any of them!

'Come on and we'll get a bag of chips, lads,' suggested Danny. He was getting fed up.

'Fair enough,' agreed Splinter. 'There's a chipper up the road.'

* * *

On the way to the chipper the three lads were fooling around, pushing each other and laughing. Jonathon gave Danny a friendly shove, and he slipped over onto the grass at the side of the road.

'I'm after falling on something wet – if it's something disgusting I'll kill yiz!' warned Danny.

It wasn't anything disgusting – it was a plastic bag, and it was heavy. Danny opened it and showed the contents to his pals.

Jonathon put his hands up to his mouth in shock.

Splinter's reaction was a little less discreet.

'There must be *thousands* there!' he screeched at the top of his voice. 'Nice one, Danny!' celebrated Splinter, clapping his hands like a seal at feeding time in the zoo.

'We can't keep that!' insisted Jonathon.

'Finders keepers, losers weepers!' quoted Splinter.

Danny closed the bag.

'Jonathon's right, Splinter,' said Danny. 'We'll have to hand it over.'

Splinter was gutted. In that wonderful moment of madness he had already picked out his new football boots and about ten other things he would buy.

'We'll give it to your dad when we get back from the chipper,' said Jonathon to Splinter. 'He can bring it to a Garda station.'

Danny stuffed the bag of money under his jacket and they continued their journey up the road for their chips.

Outside the chipper, almost as if it was meant to be, there was a Garda car and inside it sat a huge Garda eating a battered sausage.

'Look, lads,' said Danny, and he stopped in his tracks. 'Will we give the bag to him?'

Jonathon instantly agreed.

Splinter wasn't too sure.

'I don't know if that's such a good idea, lads. He looks like a bit like Shrek!'

'I'm going to hand it over to him. Come on!' said Danny.

Just as Danny banged on the window, Jonathon's phone started ringing. It was Regina. The Garda was rolling down his window, and Splinter and Danny were explaining in loud, excited voices about what they'd found.

Jonathon knew that he had to answer his phone or his mother would get suspicious. But what if she heard Danny and recognised his voice?

Jonathon moved away from the noise.

'Hi, Mum!' greeted Jonathon. 'I'm fine! … noise?' Jonathon laughed. 'It's just a few of Sebastian's friends. We're having wrestling matches in the bedroom. … We won't break anything! … I'll ring you in the morning, Mum … OK … you too … Bye.'

Phew!

Jonathon returned to his friends and the Garda – he'd missed all the excitement of telling him about finding the bag! Apparently it had been stolen from the Kimuldridge old folks' fund-raising day a couple of days previously; the Crokes boys were only a few hours in Kimuldridge and already they were heroes.

The woman who owned the chipper came out to see what all the excitement was about, and when she heard they'd found the money, she gave them batter burgers, chips and drinks on the house. Danny, Splinter and Jonathon munched their way back to the hotel to tell everyone about their triumph!

Chapter 19

The Friendly Match

The next day, even though nobody believed a word they were saying, the three heroes were still bragging about the events of the night before as they warmed up for the match against Kimuldridge under-14s.

At last, Jonathon's chance to shine had arrived – Jimmy announced the starting line up for the friendly and Jonathon was selected to start alongside Danny in midfield.

Danny was proud to have his cousin play beside him; all the hard coaching, and now at last it was pay day.

Jimmy took his place on the line alongside the subs while the other team's manager, Mick's friend, acted as referee.

The ball was thrown in and Danny and Jonathon were straight into the action.

Danny out-muscled his slightly bigger and older opponent and knocked the ball down to Jonathon.

Jonathon was feeling a bit overwhelmed, but he got a rush of adrenaline, dropped the ball to his right foot and belted an enormous pass up field. The distance he hit the ball was phenomenal, but it was to no avail as the home team's centre full back picked it up easily and knocked it out to his right half back.

It only took a half a dozen more passes and the ball was in the back of Crokes' net.

These lads were bigger, stronger and a little more experienced than Danny's team, but that didn't stop Danny from getting stuck into them.

Almost every ball that Danny Wilde won or picked up, he passed on to Jonathon. It wasn't that he was favouring his cousin over the rest of his team mates, but just that Danny knew that this game was a perfect opportunity for

Jonathon to pick up experience and get the feel for action. Training and practising were certainly necessary, but real match practice was priceless.

Crokes' were losing the game by two goals and four points to four points with only ten minutes left to the full time whistle when Jonathon made a bursting run in behind the centre full back.

Splinter had caught a super pass from Danny and fisted it to Doyler who had run in behind him, along the left wing.

Danny let a roar to Doyler to release the ball quick.

Doyler turned his marker and knocked the ball across the goal.

The gods of GAA must have been smiling down at Jonathon Wilde as he slid across the box and stretched out his right foot and toed the ball through the legs of the Kimuldridge keeper and into the net.

Jimmy missed the goal because he had been

talking to some people on the side line with microphones and television cameras.

'Perfect!' said one of the camera guys. 'That will make a great clip.'

The woman who owned the chipper had been so impressed with the three boys' honesty that she'd contacted the media. They immediately contacted Garda Doyle and when he confirmed the story, a TV van set out for the small town of Kimuldridge to capture the story of the three friends who had found the stolen money. They thought it would be a great piece of local colour for The News. And now Jonathon was on film scoring a goal for Littlestown Crokes in the sunny coast of Wexford when he should have been at Trinity Dawson's house!

As soon as the referee blew the full time whistle, all the players ran over to get in on the action.

When Jimmy ran over and told Danny and Jonathon that the media wanted to interview them for The News, Jonathon panicked and disappeared from sight.

Danny followed him. He knew that this was a serious threat to 'Operation Larry'!

Splinter, however, couldn't resist the media attention. He answered all their questions, but made sure to keep Jonathon out of his answers, not that it would make any difference.

The media and a bewildered Jimmy tried to find Danny and Jonathon, but the two boys had already hurried back to their hotel room, and as the footage was being broadcast the same day, the TV crew gave up the search and left.

* * *

Jimmy kept hassling Danny and Jonathon all the way home on the coach, but the two boys remained silent.

'I don't understand yiz at all!' said Jimmy. 'They only wanted to ask a few questions for the news. You're heroes. Ah well at least they said they'd show your goal, J.'

Those words pierced Jonathon's heart like a

dagger. He just looked at Danny with his eyes filled with tears.

Danny had no words of wisdom for his cousin this time. He knew as well as Jonathon that 'Operation Larry' was well and truly over and it was time to face the music.

When the coach arrived back at Littlestown Lawns, Danny and Jonathon kept to their plan.

Danny walked one way while his cousin walked in the opposite direction. It seemed like a pointless exercise to the boys to keep up the act, but they still had a glimmer of hope that everything would be okay.

That glimmer of hope was quickly wiped out for Jonathon as his phone began to ring. It wasn't 'Mum' that flashed on the screen this time, but 'Dad'.

'Danny! Wait up!' called Jonathon.

Danny ran back and the two boys looked at the phone as it rang and rang.

'You better answer it,' said Danny.

'No way!' said Jonathon.

'He might not know yet.'

'He must!' cried Jonathon. 'Father *never* rings me!'

The phone stopped ringing. Larry had given up, for the moment. All the worries that Jonathon had about his father knowing were confirmed as the two boys reluctantly made their way to the bus stop.

'There's Mick Wilde's son!' called a woman from one of the gardens to her next door neighbour.

The two women started clapping and cheering.

'Can we have your autographs, boys? We're proud of yiz. And, young fella, your goal looked great on the news!'

'Operation Larry' was definitely out in the open.

Danny and Jonathon and Splinter were now celebrities, and that was very, very bad news for the cousins. Danny worried about his dad finding out and Jonathon couldn't get Lowry's words out of his head – *When Father finds out you're all going to be crucified.*

The two cousins decided to go back to Aylesbridge Close to face Larry's wrath together.

Chapter 20

Big Trouble

When the boys approached the house they saw that Larry's Bentley was in the driveway.

No sooner had their shoes made their first crunch on the driveway than the hall door opened and Regina stormed out.

'Inside you two. Jonathon, you're in big trouble with your father, young man.'

She blanked Danny.

Larry was pacing up and down the lounge with a double brandy in his hand, when the boys walked in.

Danny being Danny, tried to explain to Larry that it was all his idea, but Larry wasn't having any of it. As far as he was concerned,

Danny wasn't even in the room.

Danny's heart went out to his cousin as he watched Larry deal with his son.

Jonathon was in tears.

Danny couldn't watch any more of this. Although he dreaded his own father finding out about their antics, he knew that Mick would have at least tried to talk to him, and would have given him the chance to explain.

Just as Danny turned to leave the room, the door bell rang and Regina opened it.

Danny Wilde's heart skipped two beats when he saw who walked into the hall.

Even with a walking stick in hand and Trinity's mother by his side supporting him, Mick Wilde looked taller and stronger to Danny than he ever had before.

'Dad!' sighed Danny and he ran over and threw his arms around Mick.

Larry was still in full swing in the lounge as Mick slowly, but assertively, walked towards the room.

'Stay here, son,' he said to Danny, 'I've old business to take care of with your uncle.'

The second Mick appeared in the lounge there was instant silence, almost as if somebody had flicked a switch and turned Larry off.

Mick was angry when he saw the state that his nephew was in.

'Go on out to your mammy, Jonathon. Me and your daddy are going have a little chat.'

Jonathon didn't look for his father's approval this time as he rushed out of the room.

Mick raised his walking stick and pushed the door closed.

'You've no business in this house,' growled Larry.

Mick didn't answer straight away. He just stood there with his piercing eyes fixed on his brother's.

'What happened to you, Larry?' asked Mick.

Larry just huffed and picked up his drink.

'You're putting your son through torture because of what? Something that happened between us when we were kids. Well, I'm sorry, Larry. Is that what you want to hear?'

'Don't flatter yourself, Mick. How I raise my children is my business, and it's nothing to do with you.'

'Don't worry, Larry, I didn't drag myself out of hospital to come here and tell you how to raise that boy. But what I will tell you, is that you've got a wonderful kid there. Good God, Larry, he's a national hero on the news, and here you are tearing ribbons out of him!'

'The boy disrespected me and he disrespected my rules. He needs to know the difference between right and wrong.'

Mick couldn't believe what he was hearing. Larry sounded as if he was in a courtroom instead of his home.

'He needs to be happy, you dirty-lookin' eejit, and if playing football for Littlestown Crokes makes him happy, what's the big deal?'

'What would you know about Jonathon's happiness. That boy wants for nothing.'

'Wants for nothing, you say. Is that why he was playing football behind your back?'

Larry was about to leave the room.

'Stay where you are,' insisted Mick. 'You're not running this time.'

'I don't have to take this rubbish from you.'

'Do you hate me that much, Larry? Are you so content with your mansion and fast car and your fast life that you don't have a drop of compassion for your own flesh and blood?'

'I don't need you or your kind in my life, Mick. Now get out and take your son with you.'

Mick turned away and opened the door.

'When my wife died, do you know what made the pain worse?' A tear rolled down Mick's face. 'My own brother wasn't there for me when I needed him most. Don't take Danny away from Jonathon, your son will resent you for it.'

Mick closed the door behind him.

Regina was sitting on the stairs being comforted by Trinity's mother. She was in floods of tears. The thought of the two brothers hating each other so much really upset her.

'Come on, Danny, let's get Heffo. There's a taxi waiting outside, we're going home, son.'

Jonathon walked over to his cousin and gave him a hug and banged him on the back.

'Thanks, Danny,' he whispered. 'Good luck against Barnfield.'

Chapter 21

The Final Game

Even though Danny Wilde was thrilled that his dad was home and delighted to be a local celebrity, he just couldn't get Jonathon out of his head. Every single one of the seven days leading up to the last game of the season, he missed his cousin.

It was 8 November, judgement day, and nearly everyone from Littlestown Lawns surrounded the Little Croker to support their local heroes' team.

It had only been seven weeks since the last home game, back before Mick had his stroke, when Danny had his one moment alone, standing at the side of the Little Croker. But so many things had changed for Danny in that short time. The pitch was surrounded by hundreds of supporters, Danny had Mick back by his side and it wasn't football that occupied his mind, but Jonathon.

Jimmy had all the players in their gear and ready for Mick's return to the dressing room.

Barnfield were going through their motions in the away dressing room. The chants they were making were chilling.

'Are yiz ready?' asked Jimmy as Heffo peeped his head in around the dressing room door.

The door opened.

The boys of Littlestown Crokes rose to their feet and clapped as their manager walked in. To Mick, it was like coming home.

Mick was just about to begin his pre-match talk when Danny jumped up and cheered.

'Jonathon!'

His cousin was standing outside the dressing room with Larry by his side.

'Go on, son,' said Larry, and he nodded to Mick.

'Care to join us?' smiled Mick.

Larry shook his head and smiled back.

'There's only room in that dressing room for one counsel. See you on the line.'

Anto Farrell stood up and took the number eight jersey off and handed it to Jonathon.

'Here, J,' he said.

Anto's voluntary, selfless action brought it all home to Mick why he loved GAA so much. His team was a family, his family, and now his brother had returned to his family and that made his years of dedication to the sport worthwhile.

*   *   *

'Right, home team!' called the referee. Mick hadn't delivered his talk yet.

Mick looked all around the room stopping to make eye contact with each and every one of his players.

'I'm proud of you all, lads. Today is all about you, boys. You've worked so hard for this day.

Just go out there and enjoy the game – you're already winners in my book.'

The Barnfield players made as much noise as they could passing Mick's dressing room.

Mick raised the tempo.

'Right lads! To your feet,' yelled Mick and he blew hard on his whistle.

At the top of his voice, Mick Wilde roared, 'When you go out onto that pitch boys, where are you playing?'

'The Little Croker!' replied the team.

'I can't hear you!' yelled Mick.

'THE LITTLE CROKER!' repeated his boys with extra vigour.

'And how are we going to play this last game?'

'*LIKE THE ALL-IRELAND FINAL*!!!' came the reply.

'Then get out there and win that title!'

*　　*　　*

Larry took his place among the crowd to watch

his son and Mick's son line up together in the centre of the same football pitch that he and his brother grew up playing on.

Mick just stood with his arms folded, relaxed, but the second the referee threw the ball up in the air he roared, 'Come on the Crokes!'

The crowd got behind him and started cheering for their team.

Danny Wilde jumped against Deco Savage for the opening throw in of the final game of the under-13's league. Deco was well known as a dirty player, and in fact had badly fouled Danny when Littlestown played Barnfield in the Cup Final during the summer.

Savage beat Danny to the ball and passed it back to his number nine, but Jonathon was all fired up with the thoughts of his father watching from the sideline.

Jonathon robbed the ball from the Barnfield midfielder and charged towards goal. If there was one talent that Danny had noticed in his cousin it was that he had the ability to kick the ball long and accurate.

The new Littlestown Crokes' number eight kicked an enormous pass up to Doyler who had switched back to centre half forward. Doyler collected the ball, turned his marker and kicked it along the ground towards Barry Sweeney at full forward. The number fourteen clipped the ball up into his hands and while facing away from goal he cheekily knocked it over his head for a wonderful point.

Splinter spotted Sean Dempsey and his dad watching from the Barnfield supporter's line. They didn't look too happy. Splinter smiled cheekily in their direction, as if to say, *Who's sorry now?*

The Barnfield goalkeeper made a blunder of his kick out and Crokes right full forward, Jason Delaney, took full advantage.

The number thirteen sent the ball back across the box. Splinter had left his marker sleeping and ran in behind Barry Sweeney and his marker. The keeper made an attempt to clear the ball, but Splinter dived at his feet and blocked the clearance. Doyler's right boot was the next thing to make contact with the ball sending it into the net.

GOAL!

The home crowd cheered as all the Crokes' players celebrated.

Jimmy danced around Mick.

'Here we go!' he laughed

'Hold your horses, Jimmy!' smiled Mick. There was a long way to go yet!

Barnfield were in shock with the bombardment from Crokes. Their manager hurled instructions at them to get them to lift their game.

It worked!

Danny's team and Jimmy were to pay for their premature celebrations.

Mick was right! The Crokes' manager knew just how good Barnfield were, after all they had beaten his team in the cup final.

Barnfield upped their game to an

outstanding level.

They plundered the home team's half of the pitch for every ball and by the time the referee blew his whistle for half time, Littlestown Crokes were trailing by a score of 1-2 to 0-7.

Larry moved closer down the line at half-time to get a closer look at Mick in action with the boys.

Mick's boys looked ragged as he delivered his half-time talk.

'We're going to have to up the pace again from the throw in, lads,' encouraged Mick. 'And look for each other. Darren and Karl, try and pick out a player with your passes rather than just knocking the ball anywhere.'

Mick was talking to his half-backs.

Larry had noticed that too. The ball was being given back to Barnfield every time Crokes worked hard to break their attacks down, and that was putting extra strain on the team.

Mick made two changes for the second half

to try and inject a boost of pace, with fresh legs.

Both teams took their positions and the referee threw the ball up in the air.

This time Jonathon jumped for the throw-in against Deco Savage.

The Crokes' number eight could feel the ball touching his right hand when, *CLATTER!* Savage caught Jonathon in the ear with his elbow, just as he had to Danny in the cup final.

The referee blew hard on his whistle as Jonathon fell to the ground, holding his head. There was blood.

Danny pushed Savage to the ground.

'Just because you're *called* Savage doesn't mean you have to *act* that way too!'

'Get in there, Jimmy!' instructed Mick. Larry ran after Jimmy, and Mick followed Larry as quick as his legs would take him.

There was pandemonium in the centre of the field between Larry and Barnfield's manager as Mick and Jimmy tended to Jonathon.

Deco Savage wanted to go for Danny for

pushing him to the ground, but he was quickly ushered out of the way.

Jonathon wasn't hurt as badly as first expected. His ear was cut, so Jimmy wrapped a bandage around his head to cover the wound.

By the time the referee restored order and sent all non-players back to their lines, a good ten minutes was already gone on the clock and there hadn't even been one kick of the ball.

To the delight of Barnfield and utter disgust of Littlestown, Deco Savage got off without even a warning as the referee concluded that it was injury by accident. Deco was just going for the ball.

Total rubbish! thought Danny.

Once again the ball was thrown high in the air. Jonathon wasn't jumping for a second helping of Savage's elbow so Danny gladly stepped in.

Savage made a clean challenge this time as he knew that a repeat of his tricks would get him the red card.

Danny leapt high and won the ball fair and square, knocking it and his opponent to the ground. Just like the first day Danny Wilde had passed the ball to his cousin outside their granny's flat, Jonathon passed the ball back to Danny and the Crokes' captain went on a Danny solo, leaving the Savage eating dirt.

Barnfield's centre half back charged out at Danny leaving Doyler unmarked.

Danny lobbed the ball over his head and into the path of Doyler, then Danny raced past the centre half back in support of Doyler.

Barry Sweeney, Crokes' full forward pulled the centre full back wide, opening the way to goal for Doyler, but Doyler panicked and hit the ball wide of the posts.

No score!

That's the way it was for the next fifteen minutes of the game. Every time Danny or Jonathon won the ball in midfield and sent it up the field, Crokes' forward line wasted their chances.

Only for the two Wilde boys getting stuck in,

Barnfield probably would have increased their lead, but they hadn't scored either and the gap remained at two points in Barnfield's favour as the remaining minutes closed in.

Mick, Jimmy and Larry were pumping sweat on the line and to make matters worse, Tommy and Sean Dempsey were now standing beside them and taunting them.

Crokes were on the attack as Splinter belted down the line chasing a long ball from his left half forward.

Danny knew that this was their last chance so he and Jonathon headed into the Barnfield goal area in anticipation of a ball in from Splinter.

The tension on the home team's line was boiling over as Tommy Dempsey kept shouting at the referee to blow up.

Never before had Mick Wilde seen Jimmy Murphy lose his temper, but Tommy had his nerves gone. Jimmy turned to Tommy just as his son sent a piercing low ball across the goal mouth.

'If you don't shut–'

Jimmy never got to finish that sentence because at that split second, everybody along the Littlestown line roared the same word.

'PENALTY!'

Barry Sweeney had picked up Splinter's pass and just as he was about to shoot, who was there to take his legs from under him? Deco Savage.

The crowd moved up the line towards the goal.

Danny asked the referee for the ball.

'What's left, ref?' asked the captain.

The referee smiled.

'This will be the last kick of the game.'

Danny's heart was racing. He knew that it had to be a goal if they were to take the title.

Jimmy, Mick and Larry were now chewing on their fingers.

'I can't watch, Mick!' said Jimmy, turning away.

If Jimmy was nervous with the thought of the team's star player taking the all-important last kick of the season, then he was surely ready for a stretcher as Danny Wilde shocked everyone by throwing the ball to Jonathon.

'You can do it, J!' said Danny.

Half of the Crokes' players had to turn away, like Jimmy.

Jonathon nervously placed the ball on the spot. His legs were like jelly.

'Okay, goalkeeper?' asked the referee.

The goalkeeper nodded.

The whistle blew.

'Okay, Eight! When you're ready.'

Jonathon Wilde slowly walked back from the ball for his run up.

He took in a big breath of air and fixed his eyes on one spot in the goal. That was his target.

'Go on, son!' roared Larry from the side line.

THUMP!

The ball left Jonathon's boot and rocketed towards the goal and smashed into the top right hand corner of the net.

The title was Crokes'!

All the Crokes players lifted Jonathon up in the air as the pitch was invaded by all the local supporters.

When Mick and Jimmy were finished hugging and congratulating each other, Jimmy let Heffo off his lead and ran with the home team's mascot onto the pitch.

Larry put his hand out to shake Mick's.

'Congratulations.'

'Thanks to your son!' smiled Mick and the handshake turned into a hug.

Danny and Jonathon left the celebration to join their dads. There was a tall bearded man talking to Mick.

'Danny,' smiled Mick. 'I want you to meet Mr Jenkins.'

Mick had rung Mr Jenkins the week before the final game and explained why Danny had missed his training session with the development squad. Mr Jenkins agreed to come and watch the game, but Mick thought it would be best if he didn't say anything to Danny just in case it interfered with his game.

'Great game, Danny,' said Mr Jenkins and he reached out to shake Danny Wilde's hand.

Then Mr Jenkins turned towards Jonathon.

'And you must be Jonathon, Danny's cousin.'

Larry had been proudly bragging about his son.

'It's clear to see after that game that talent runs in the Wilde family! We've another training session coming up soon, boys, and I'd like if both of you could be there,' continued Mr Jenkins, then he smiled, and looked at Mick, 'I'll be in touch,' he said, and bid them farewell.

Danny and Jonathon rejoined the celebrations with the rest of the team knowing in their hearts that this victorious day was just the beginning of great days ahead, for all the Wilde boys, on the Little Croker.

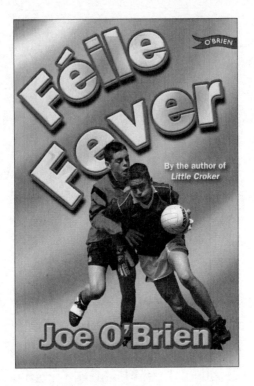

Danny Wilde and his teammates are finding the Under-14s Division tough going. They've lost one of their best goal-scorers to injury and it looks like they'll have no chance of winning the County Féile!

Could Todd, the new Australian kid, be the answer to their prayers? Todd's an Aussie Rules player – tough and skilful – but can he become a real GAA player in time?

It's all to play for in the second book about GAA player Danny Wilde.

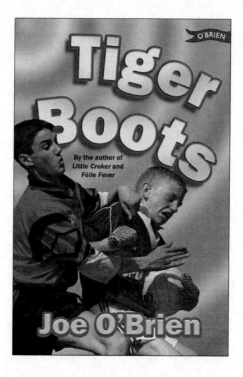

The Crokes are doing well at football this season and are hoping to finish ahead of rivals Barntown in the League. But things aren't going as well in Danny's personal life; his dad, Mick, the Croke's coach, is having a hard time - he's worried about losing his job, and his oldest friends' daughter, Clara, is sick and needs an expensive operation. But GAA is like one big family, and when Danny and the Crokes hear that Clara is the captain of her GAA team in Boston, USA they're determined to raise money for her. Though there are a few hitches along the way - like trouble with Trinity, the girl he has his eye on - between training, school and a fundraising football marathon, Danny and the Crokes make this a season to remember!